NEVER DOUBT MY LOVE

On holiday in Paris, Lisa meets and falls in love with Luke. They marry and go to live in the family château near Grenoble, where Lisa encounters Frédérique Legrand. Frédérique tells her that Luke had asked her to marry him but that she had refused, not wanting to take on responsibility for Luke's orphaned cousin, Jamie. Now, she warns, she intends to get him back — at any price!

DAISY THOMSON

NEVER DOUBT MY LOVE

Complete and Unabridged

LINFORD
Leicester

First published in Great Britain in 1985 by
Robert Hale Limited
London

First Linford Edition
published December 1994
by arrangement with
Robert Hale Limited
London

British Library CIP Data

Thomson, Daisy
    Never doubt my love.—Large print ed.—
    Linford romance library
    I. Title II. Series
    823.914 [F]

    ISBN 0–7089–7623–9

Published by
F. A. Thorpe (Publishing) Ltd.
Anstey, Leicestershire

Set by Words & Graphics Ltd.
Anstey, Leicestershire
Printed and bound in Great Britain by
T. J. Press (Padstow) Ltd., Padstow, Cornwall

This book is printed on acid-free paper

1

I WATCHED with amusement as the small boy fumbled to adjust the sails of the yacht which was almost as big as he was. His father was watching him too, an affectionate expression on his face as he wisely waited to be asked to lend a hand.

The boy, intent on his task, the father's interest centred on the boy, made an appealing picture. I took my camera from its case and focused it on them. This was the kind of moment I like to capture on film. Natural, unposed, it would be perfect for the family album, except that in this case it wouldn't feature in that album, for I could hardly walk up to a strange man and say to him,

'Excuse me. I've just taken a picture of you and your son. If you will let me

1

have your address, I'll post a copy on to you.'

He would think I was either touting for business, as other photographers in the garden were doing, or that I was blatantly trying to pick him up.

I continued idly to watch the pair as together they finally managed to get the sails set to the little boy's liking, then with the man hooking a restraining finger round the elastic band at the back waist of his short pants, the child leaned well over the edge of the octagonal pond and pushed the yacht out to join the other small craft already on the water, craft which a sudden gusty autumn breeze sent skittering from one side of the pond to the other.

The same breeze carried to my ears the boy's shout of excitement as his ship sailed smartly away, and I was surprised to hear him shout in English, "Luke, it's going right to the other side. Let's run round and get it."

Thank goodness, I smiled to myself

that I hadn't gone up to the stranger and asked for his address to send the photograph to, for I would have addressed him in French, and an Englishman, in Paris, would most definitely have believed I was up to no good.

On the advice of my doctor, I was taking a late holiday. A bout of flu had left me not so much depressed as restless and unsure of myself. My father, for whom I work, had backed up the doctor's suggestion, although he ascribed my restlessness not so much to post flu depression as to what he termed a late spring fever.

"I've been watching you, Lisa," he had said. "You have been getting restless for months. It is time you got away for a break. This is a quiet month in the studio. There isn't a rush for graduation portraits or wedding photographs. I shall be able to cope with what orders we have for family portraits and the like. You have had some success recently with travel magazines, so why not go to France or Italy and take some photographs of out of the way places as you wander around. That would make your break the more interesting."

The idea appealed. I had been toying for some time with the idea of doing something different, yet I hadn't wanted to let my father down by leaving him to cope on his own. I also knew the place I would like to wander round and photograph. Paris. My year at the Sorbonne had given me an opportunity to get to know it.

Another gust of wind whipped more leaves from the trees. A large golden leaf came dancing towards me. I watched it for a moment, and then smiling at my own childishness, I made a grab at it, missed, and then tried again. With an exclamation of triumph I caught it and carefully placed it in a compartment of my shoulder bag. I was being silly. I knew it. But when I had been a child someone had told me that it was good luck to catch a falling autumn leaf and

I could do with a little luck, a fillip to bring me out of my restless mood, something that would point me in a more exciting direction.

As I zipped up my bag I glanced once more towards the pond, to find that the man who had earlier attracted my attention was looking directly at me, an expression of amusement on his face. He made no attempt to avoid my glance, and his continued look made me blush. What an idiot I must have seemed to him, prancing round like a six year old in my efforts to catch the leaf. And yet, I decided, it wasn't a supercilious smile on the man's face. It was more a smile which implied that he knew about the old superstition and was wishing me luck with my catch. It was a smile which, after that first moment of embarrassment made me smile back at him as if he was someone I knew, a smile which would have charmed a response from even the dourest female.

I wanted to go on smiling at him.

I was overcome by the strangest feeling. It was as if I was being physically drawn towards the man, and the feeling was so strong I actually took a step forward before I had time to pull myself together and avert my gaze, concentrating my attention on replacing my bag over my shoulder before deliberately moving away in the direction of the gateway to the Boulevard Saint-Michel.

I had only taken a few steps when I heard a child scream with rage. I turned in time to see a couple of multi-coloured haired adoloscents seize the yacht from the little boy who had first attracted my attention. They pushed him roughly to the ground and made off, laughing and shouting and shoving aside the other children as they headed in my direction to make for the exit from the park.

I was so angry I acted without thinking. As they came up behind me, ready to push me out of their way

6

as they had done to others who had tried to intercept them, I quickly side-stepped, put out a foot, tripped up the nearer youth, sending him sprawling on his knees, then slung my heavy camera case at the face of the other youth who was holding the yacht.

The unexpected blow on his cheek made him yelp with pain and drop the boat. By this time several students had joined in the chase, and I left them to go after the two young thieves while I stooped down and retrieved the yacht, and turned back to the pond, where the little boy was crying pitifully for his mother, while the man tried at one and the same time to calm him down and staunch the flow of blood which was welling from a knee which had been cut when the child had been pushed to the ground.

"I want mummy. I want mummy." The wail was heartbreaking and shrill and constant and rising to hysteria. People were staring at the pair, embarrassing the man with their muttered comments as I came up to them.

"It's all right, young man. I've got your yacht back. Look!" I said briskly, but he paid no more attention to me than he was doing to his father. Instead of looking, he pressed himself more tightly against the man's expensive navy cords.

"There, there, Jamie," the man said gently. "You are all right. The cut isn't as deep as all the bleeding makes it appear to be." He ruffled the boy's hair and shot me an appealing look, obviously out of his depth as to how to handle the wailing child, and added, hopefully. "The lady has brought the yacht back and there's been no damage done, so everything is quite all right now."

"Of course it is, Jamie," I said softly and knelt down beside him, to be nearer his height. Gently putting my hand on his shoulder I added. "You know, you are much too big a boy to keep on crying like this. A really brave boy wouldn't make such a fuss about

8

a tiny little cut like the one you have on your knee."

This time I got through to him. Perhaps it was my woman's voice which soothed him. Perhaps he even thought his mother had arrived. His crying ceased, he drew away from the man and turned to look at me. I put an arm round him and gave him a reassuring cuddle.

"There you are," I held the yacht out to him with my free hand, and hurried on before the tearful gulps could become a cry again, "I did get your yacht back, and what's more," I tried to coax a smile, "Do you know, I gave the bullies who took it a spanking?"

The words held his attention and made him look at me, tears still in his eyes, lower lip still trembling.

I pressed home my advantage. "They didn't like it so they have run away, and now I have come to patch up those scratches of yours. If you will give your father the boat to hold, perhaps you can help me unzip my bag and find the box of plasters I have in it?" I slipped the bag from my shoulder and handed it to him.

I had held his interest as I had hoped to. Small children seem to be fascinated by handbags, and Jamie was no exception. He took the satchel and pulled the zip open with such gusto that some of the things I had stuffed into it came tumbling out and fell onto the gritty ground. The rosy apple I had bought for my picnic lunch rolled past my feet. The paper bag containing a couple of crusty rolls split open as it hit the ground and its contents were covered with sand.

In his dismay the little boy dropped the bag, and all else in it scattered over the ground, including the 'lucky' chestnut leaf.

"I'm sorry, I'm sorry!" Jamie's voice rose once more to a wail of anguish. "I didn't mean to do that."

"Of course you didn't," I gave him a quick hug. "It was an accident.

But let's get everything packed into the bag again, before the wind blows them away. Except for the plasters of course. We'll need those. Perhaps your father will help?" I suggested, smiling up at the man beside us.

He frowned, shook his head, and said softly as Jamie went off to retrieve the apple which had rolled a few feet away.

"I'm not Jamie's father. I'm his uncle, and," the frown changed to a smile, "You can have no idea how grateful I am that you came to the rescue just now. I'm not used to dealing with crises like this, though I shall have to learn how to," he shook his head and sighed, then, glancing at his watch said, with another shake of his head.

"I wouldn't have had to try to deal with this particular one either, if my sister had arrived here on time, but being on time is not one of Marguerite's strong points."

By now Jamie had stuffed everything higgeldy piggeldy back into the satchel and zipped it shut.

"I remembered to keep the tin of plasters out," he said proudly.

"But you forgot to pack one very important item, Jamie," smiled the man, bending down to pick up the chestnut leaf.

He reopened the bag and placed it carefully inside before turning to me, eyes as well as mouth smiling. "I couldn't let you lose your good luck charm because of us, could I?"

I responded to his teasing glance and replied lightly.

"It's a pity Jamie didn't catch a leaf, then he might not have fallen. Come along young man," I took the little boy by the hand. "We had better clean up those scratches of yours without further delay, and you can choose the plaster you want to put over the cut. There is a bench further along the path where you can sit while I do what is necessary."

Jamie shot me an anxious look. "It won't hurt, will it?"

I ignored the question, and to divert

his attention I said.

"Do you know, Jamie, we are presently walking along the same path where a famous poet called Theóphile Gautier used to take his pet lobster for a walk on a leash. You know what a lobster is, don't you?" I prattled on, trying to keep him from thinking of his knee, for he was limping quite noticeably, which surprised me, for I wouldn't have thought the grazing, nasty though it was, or even the small cut from which blood was still oozing would have made him walk so haltingly. Of course, it was quite possible that he was doing what children very often do, making his hurt seem worse than it was, to claim attention.

"I know what a lobster is," he assured me. "We sometimes have them for dinner at home. I think they taste horrible, but grandmother likes them."

"I had never heard that story about Gautier," his uncle looked at me with deepening interest. "Is it true, or are you making it up?"

"It's quite true, or at least, it's recorded in several guide books, and when I was at the Sorbonne, a fellow student tried to see if he could get a lobster to walk with him down this path. It caused quite a sensation."

The man looked at me askance. "If you were at the Sorbonne, you must speak French quite well."

"I suppose I do," I shrugged. "At one time I thought of teaching it."

"I speak French too, and so does Uncle Lulu," put in Jamie.

I guessed he was bragging a bit and smiled, not so much for his boasting, but because the name Lulu did not seem to fit the ruggedly handsome man who was walking alongside us.

We came to a vacant bench and I told Jamie to sit down and open the box of plasters carefully, while I myself opened my bag again to take out a box of cleansing tissues and the large, rosy apple.

"Here you are, Jamie," I handed him

the apple. "The tissues may sting a little when I wipe your knee, so you bite hard into the apple while I'm removing the grit. It will stop you crying out."

"That's the first time I have heard of an apple being used as an anaesthetic," his uncle joked. "You will have to tell Aunt Marguerite about it," he went on putting a firm hand on the boy's shoulder.

"I'll have to tell her about the lobster too," giggled Jamie.

"First of all, you will bite into that apple," I ordered, and waited to hear his teeth crunch into the pulp before I started firmly and swiftly to wipe the sandy grit from the cut. He flinched at the sting of the lotion, but his mouth was too full for him to be able to cry out, and by the time he had swallowed the large mouthful he had bitten out, the most painful part of the cleansing operation was over.

He happily munched at the fruit while I placed a plaster carefully over the cut, and by the time I had done this and wiped the dried blood which had earlier trickled down his leg, he had eaten more than half of the fruit.

"I hope that hasn't spoilt his appetite for lunch," I turned to his uncle, who had been watching my swift first aid with admiring eyes.

"It would take more than an apple to take the edge of Jamie's appetite," he assured me. "What's more," he looked at me directly, "It isn't Jamie's lunch that has been spoilt, it has been yours. You were planning a picnic in the gardens, weren't you? That's why you had those rolls and an apple and that bar of Meunier chocolate in your satchel, isn't it?"

I nodded.

"Well, now you have no apple. The rolls which Jamie stuffed back into your bag are too dirty to eat, and — "

"And I've still got my bar of chocolate," I said lightly. "In any case, now that the wind has become so strong, it would be much too cold

16

to enjoy an al fresco meal," I popped the tin of plasters back into my bag. "A nice hot dish of onion soup would be much more appealing."

I looked down at Jamie who was still sitting on the bench, holding his leg out to see how big a plaster I had put on it.

"You were a very good patient," I told him, "but in future, make sure you don't trip over your feet again. "And here," I delved among the other contents to take the gritty rolls from the satchel. "You can take these and feed the sparrows under the trees over there. That will give you something to do until your aunt comes along."

I looked from him to his uncle.

"I do hope your sister turns up before that black cloud overhead deluges the park, and I also hope you will have no more mishaps to-day," I smiled and slipped my bag back over my shoulder beside the camera case. "Good-bye. Have a lovely holiday in Paris."

I was about to walk away, but the

man put out his hand and caught hold of my arm.

"My dear girl, you can't walk off like that after what you have done for us, can she Jamie?" he appealed to his nephew. "The very least we can do is invite you to join us for lunch, especially when," he smiled at me with that smile I had found so attractive the first time he had looked at me, "yes, especially when we were responsible for ruining yours."

"You will join us, won't you?" he cajoled. "It will be our way of saying 'Thank you' for all your help."

"I was only too glad to help."

"And I was more than glad of your assistance, so please, let me express my appreciation for what you have done by taking you for lunch."

I hesitated. I had been in Paris for almost a week. The friends I had hoped to visit in the city were presently out of town, and I had been getting rather tired of my own company. It would make a pleasant change to lunch with someone, have someone to talk to, but this man was, after all, a stranger and I might find a further hour or two in his company trying. In any case, I doubted if he really expected me to take him up on his invitation. He had only issued it out of a sense of obligation, and could already be regretting his words.

He sensed my hesitation and said quickly.

"Jamie won't be our only chaperone, if that is what is worrying you. My sister will be joining us at any moment. She has more sense than to keep me waiting for more than quarter of an hour," he added, glancing at his watch.

He waited for my answer, but still I hesitated. The sensible thing to do was to shake my head and say politely but firmly that I couldn't accept, that he owed me nothing for what little I had done to help, say 'Good-bye' and walk away, but at heart I didn't want to do the sensible thing. I wanted to spend a little more time with this man whom I found so attractive. Yet that was being foolish, I scolded myself. I mustn't let an emotional instinct over-ride my common sense.

I was about to open my mouth to say the words which would mean the final parting of our ways, but the coaxing smile on the man's lips, the pleading look in Jamie's eyes, weakened my resolve.

Instead of refusing, I found myself responding to that smile and saying, little realising how this decision was to alter the course of my life.

"You are not leaving me with any excuses for turning your invitation down, are you?"

"None at all," he agreed, the satisfied smile of a man who has got his own way quirking his lips. "So, now that that is settled, Jamie," he held out a hand to his nephew to pull him to his feet, "Let's go and see if we can find this aunt of yours."

The words were hardly out of his mouth when a woman's voice called.

"There you are! I was quite worried when you weren't at the pond when I arrived. You are always so punctual I thought something must have happened to you. Luckily I spotted Jamie and that yacht of his when I glanced along this path and," she stopped abruptly, her eyes fixed on the plaster on the boy's knee, then continued in an anxious voice.

"Jamie, you've hurt your knee again. How did that happen?"

"It's rather an involved story, Marguerite," her brother replied. "I'll explain what happened over lunch. My friend here will be joining us, by the way."

Marguerite, a lovely red-head, looked at me, her forehead wrinkled in a puzzled frown, as she became aware for the first time that I was with her brother and nephew.

"Let me introduce you to," he paused, grinned, and went on, "to Florence Nightingale."

"Florence Nightingale?" Marguerite

echoed the name, staring at me with disbelief. "That isn't really your name, is it?"

I giggled. "No. It isn't. I'm Lisa Angus."

"Lisa Angus," Jamie's uncle repeated my name. "Now that I know who you are, may I make the usual introductions? Lisa, this is my sister Marguerite Fletcher. I am Luke Fletcher, and Jamie is Jamie de la Haie."

Jamie promptly held out his hand to acknowledge the introduction, and I shook it solemnly, all the while conscious that his aunt was watching me with a puzzled look on her face.

"Luke," she spoke sharply. "I don't understand what's going on," her eyes strayed to the plaster on Jamie's knee. "It wasn't by any chance Miss Angus who is responsible for Jamie's injury?"

"Far from it, Maggie," I winced at Luke's corruption of his sister's attractive name. "Quite the opposite, in fact. Lisa came to our rescue, didn't she, Jamie?" he ruffled his nephew's hair. "We've invited her to join us for lunch as a way of showing our gratitude."

Noting the slight frown on the other woman's face I said quickly.

"I've told your brother there is no need to thank me like that."

"But there is," he spoke with determination. "I like to pay my debts."

"What he means is that he doesn't like to be beholden to anyone," said his sister drily. "You might as well accept the invitation gracefully. Luke likes to get his own way, and he usually does," she grimaced at her brother. "In any case, if there is a story to be told, as I gather there is, I would like to hear your version as well as his."

"Now," she added, the crispness of her tone reminding me of her brother, "We had better be on our way. I have parked the car as near as I could to the entrance gate, but waiting is limited, and I can't afford another fine this week."

"It's just as well you are going to marry someone who can afford to pay your fines for you," joked Luke, taking hold of Jamie's free hand and walking towards the gate.

"It will be some time before Edouard will be doing that," she snapped. "There is no way I can talk him into agreeing to the conditions that were set and I can see his point of view. Luke, it would be so much easier for you and Frederique, even although she doesn't want to take on — "

"That's enough, Maggie," Luke interrupted her quickly, shooting her a warning glance.

"I'm sorry, Luke," she muttered. "I shouldn't have said that. It's just that I'm all strung up. Edouard and I had another of our hopeless arguments this morning, and I just can't see a way out at the moment. We always seem to be at loggerheads these days," she sighed. "Never fall in love, Lisa," she turned to me. "It makes one too vulnerable."

She took a set of keys from the

expensive black patent handbag she was carrying and stopped beside a scarlet Alfa Romeo which I noticed had a French registration. She unlocked the passenger door and held it open for me to get in.

I was feeling embarrassed at the flare up of a family problem and beginning to wish I had been strong-minded enough to turn down Luke's invitation, but there was nothing I could do about it now.

Jamie and his uncle slipped into the back seats, and Marguerite got behind the wheel. She was a capable driver, insinuating the car in and out of the lines of mid-day traffic with skill.

"I do hope we'll find a parking place near Lipp," she mentioned the famous brasserie on the Boulevard St. Germain. "We'll be late if we have too far to walk. It's almost one o'clock already."

There was amusement in Luke's voice as he replied.

"We'll be in plenty of time, Marguerite. Knowing your time-keeping,

I told you the table was reserved for one o'clock, but the actual reservation is for one thirty."

She made a face at him in the driving mirror.

"Ha, ha. Very clever."

"Wasn't it?" he agreed equably. "Now you have time to look for a parking space without getting hot under the collar."

Their bantering reminded me of the way my brothers and I had teased each other, and made me feel more at ease in their company.

"I'm not going to have lobster for lunch," Jamie announced suddenly from the back seat.

His aunt raised her eyebrows. "What made you say that?"

"We were talking about lobsters this morning, weren't we, Lulu? Did you know, Aunt Marguerite, that you can take lobsters for a walk on a leash, just like a dog, and I wouldn't like to eat a dog, would you?"

"Of course not," she laughed, "but

who has been stuffing your head with such nonsense? Really, Luke," she chided her brother, "you should know better."

"It's not nonsense," protested Jamie. "It was Lisa who told me." He used my name as if we were old friends.

"It's true," I answered her enquiring look and retold the story of Gautier and his unusual pet, making Marguerite laugh and say that she had certainly never heard the tale before.

"I've an idea Lisa could tell us lots of stories about Paris," said Luke. "She tells me she was a student at the Sorbonne."

"Were you indeed?" Marguerita shot me a swift sideways glance before smartly pulling into a parking space as another car pulled out. "Now, wasn't that lucky," she beamed with satisfaction, referring to finding such a convenient space and not, I guessed, to my having been a student in Paris. "We won't have far to walk after all. The restaurant is only about a hundred metres from here. I expect you have been there before?" she glanced at me again as I was unfastening my seat belt.

"I've heard of it, of course," I said with a shake of my head, "but a place like Lipp was way out of my student income."

"Mine too, when I was at the Sorbonne," Marguerite laughed. "Being a business woman and not a student makes a lot of difference."

Jamie and Luke had got out of the car and were standing on the pavement waiting for us. As I stepped up beside them a gust of wind whipped away the silk scarf I had loosely tucked into the neck of my blouse. I let out an exclamation of dismay, made a grab to retrieve it, but it was swept out of my reach towards the roadway.

Luke in turn snatched at it as it flew past his head and managed to catch it.

"Thanks," I breathed my relief and held out my hand for it, but instead of returning it, he folded it and placed it in his pocket.

"It will be safer there meantime," he decided as another, stronger gust of wind almost swept us off our feet, "and I think we shall have to make a dash for it," he added, as heavy raindrops spattered across the pavement. "Come along, Jamie," he took his nephew's hand, "Let's see if we can get to the brasserie before the girls."

There was lobster on the menu, but no one chose it. Indeed, I was more interested in glancing surreptitiously round me to see if I could spot any of the famous personalities who are said to be frequent visitors to the place than in studying the menu, and when Luke, smiling, reminded me that we had come to eat and not sightsee, I smiled back at him and asked if he would make a choice for me since he would know the specialities.

"What you mean, Lisa," he teased me, "is that you want me to choose because you are still remembering your student days when you didn't know how much the young man who took you out could afford. Isn't that right?"

I blushed, and Marguerite came to my rescue.

"Don't pay any attention to Luke, Lisa. He is a born tease, as I know only too well."

The meal was an excellent one, served unhurriedly so that there was time to enjoy both food and conversation, although the conversation tended to be one-sided, for Marguerite, having been intrigued when she learned how I had met her brother and nephew, was openly curious to find out more about me.

By the time coffee and tiny biscuits were being put in front of us, she had managed to elicit where I came from, if my parents were alive and what they did. I even found myself telling her that although I had trained to be a language teacher, when I had left college there had been too many teachers after too few jobs. After a stint of working in a school in Switzerland teaching English, I had decided to return to Edinburgh and take up my father's offer of a job in his photographic studio.

"My father had always encouraged my interest in photography, which was only natural, I suppose, and I found myself becoming more interested in it than in teaching."

"It's a family business, is it?" asked Luke, interested. "Does it go back generations, like ours?"

I wondered what his business was as I replied. "No. The studio was a new venture for my father. He was a news photographer. However he had to give that up for health reasons. The car he was in was blown up by a land mine in Lebanon, and he received back injuries which now limit his mobility."

"Your father isn't Bill Angus by any chance?" exclaimed Luke. "I saw an exhibition of his pictures the last time I was in London and thought them superb. Are you as good as he is?"

I grimaced. "I would like to be, but I

still have a long way to go. Perhaps this project I have in mind at the moment will help me decide what I want to do in future."

"What is that?"

"I've decided to do a photographic guide book of Paris from an unusual angle. I've even got a name for it. Parisian Places, Parisian Faces. You see," I went on with enthusiasm, "I know so many off beat corners of the city the ordinary tourist never visits, yet which have as much charm, and often more intriguing histories, than the better known tourist attractions."

A cat curled round our feet and Jamie stroked it.

"I like cats," he piped up. "I've got one of my very own."

"What's he called?"

"He's a she and she's called Snoopy. She's striped like a tiger and she sleeps on my bed all night. Grandmother says that shouldn't be allowed. I don't like grandmother, you know," he went on, to be interrupted sternly by Luke.

"That's enough, young man."

"But I don't. She said she was going to take Snoopy away." He paused to look at his uncle in horror. "You don't think she'll chase Snoopy away when I'm not there, do you?"

"Don't be silly, of course she won't. In any case, Nana is looking after Snoopy while you are on holiday. She wouldn't let anything happen to her. And talking of Nana," he diverted the boy's attention, "I think we might choose the present you are going to take home to her this afternoon, don't you?"

"That's a very good idea," put in Marguerite while I continued to stare at Jamie in surprise. The way he had spoken of his grandmother was unusual. Most children love them. He had stated quite seriously he disliked his and neither his uncle nor his aunt had seemed surprised at the statement.

"I think we had better leave before Jamie brings any more family skeletons out of the cupboard. We don't want to give Lisa a bad impression of our clan, do we?"

"What's a family skeleton?" asked Jamie, but Marguerite brushed aside his question to say, no longer smiling.

"I wish all our cupboards were bare of skeletons and the like. I wish we were a normal family. I wish you and I weren't trapped by that insane promise we gave to Alain." Her voice rose shrilly. "Yes, Luke, I wish to God we were free from that commitment so that I could marry Edouard. What's more," she glared at her brother, "you could do something about that if you cared for me at all, but you are so damned selfish, so taken up with your own affairs. I am quite sure Frédérique wouldn't take much persuasion to overcome her dislike of chi — "

"That's enough, Marguerite," Luke interrupted quickly before she could complete her sentence. "For goodness sake, get a grip of yourself."

"A grip?" his sister's fingers played with the large solitaire diamond on her ring finger. "How can I keep calm and smiling and serene the way things are going. I have had to postpone my wedding indefinitely. You can't imagine what that's like. The frustration, the misery, the — the — Oh God!" she gulped, and with that she pushed her chair away from the table with an abrupt movement, rose to her feet, and with tears spilling over her cheeks, went hurrying to the powder room.

I made to follow her, but Luke put out a detaining hand and said, "Leave her for a moment. Things will work out if she will only be patient."

2

I FELT embarrassed at being involved in a family scene, and was certain that Luke Fletcher must now be regretting the impulse which had prompted him to invite a stranger to join the family luncheon party.

"I think I should leave before your sister returns," I suggested. "She might be upset to find me still here."

"No, you must stay. She will be all right in a few minutes, you'll see, and she would be annoyed if she thought that her behaviour had scared you away."

"Is it because I keep calling you Lulu that Aunt Marguerite was angry?" asked Jamie anxiously. "I didn't mean to upset her."

"It was nothing to do with you," Luke assured him.

"Grandmother says I must be a

nuisance to you," Jamie looked tearful. "I heard her say to Nana that if it wasn't for me Aunt Marguerite's wedding wouldn't have had to be postponed."

"You misheard what was said," Luke spoke firmly. "What's more, young man, you shouldn't listen in to grown up conversations. Now, tell me," he adroitly changed the conversation, "do you know what your aunt has planned for us to do this afternoon?"

Jamie scowled. "We are going to meet Frédérique and then go shopping. I don't like shopping."

"I don't like it much either," agreed his uncle, giving me an amused glance over the boy's head. "However, to-day it won't be so bad, because you will have some shopping of your own to do. Have you any idea what you would like to buy Nana? Chocolates, perhaps?"

"She doesn't like chocolates," Jamie continued to pout.

"How about a china cat that looks

like Snoopy?" I suggested. "You told me your Nana was fond of cats."

"She is," agreed Jamie. "She has one of her own."

"A china cat?" Luke nodded. "That seems a good idea, doesn't it, Jamie? I am sure your aunt will know the very place to find one," he smiled as he rose to his feet, looking across the room to Marguerite who was making her way back to our table, watched by the tough-looking individual at the counter, who reminded me vaguely of a man I had noticed watching the children at the Luxembourg gardens with overmuch interest.

"Lisa, I am sorry about what happened just now," she apologised ruefully. "I hope I didn't upset you. Luke," she turned to her brother, "I hope I haven't kept you waiting too long again," her smile was bright, natural, her manner serene showing how completely she had recovered her composure. "You must have been getting anxious knowing how impatient Frédérique would be if we didn't arrive at our meeting place on time."

"Women," Luke shook his head. "It would seem it is all right for a girl to keep a man waiting, but never the other way round."

"I don't want to spend an afternoon with Frédérique," Jamie reverted to sulks. "She never pays any attention to me, so she wouldn't miss me. I'd much rather," he eyed me hopefully, "go with Lisa to choose a present for Nana."

"I daresay you would, young man," Luke's eyes twinkled with amusement, "but we have taken up quite enough of Lisa's time to-day. I am certain she is itching to be off about her own business now, although she has been politely trying to hide her impatience."

He was wrong. I wasn't itching to be about my business. The few hours I had spent with this attractive and intriguing family had made the prospect of wandering round Paris on my own again seem infinitely dreary, which was silly, considering I am usually perfectly content with my own company when working on a project.

Moreover, not for a long time had I felt myself drawn to a man as I was to Luke Fletcher. I liked the way he looked, the way he smiled. I liked the way he teased his sister and his gentleness to his nephew. I would have liked to get to know him better, but that, of course was quite unlikely. In a few minutes we would shake hands and say 'Good-bye' and that would be that.

Afraid that any hesitation to answer might make it look as if I wanted to impose myself on them, I said briskly.

"Yes. You're right. I'm afraid I must leave you now. I'm expecting a 'phone call at my hotel this afternoon, and I wouldn't like to miss it."

I followed them from the restaurant, then stopped on the pavement outside to hold my hand out for the formal good-bye handshakes.

"Thanks for the lovely lunch, and

thanks for helping me fulfil an ambition I have had since my days at the Sorbonne, that of having a meal at the Brasserie Lipp one day."

Marguerite was the first to take my hand.

"Lisa, do you live far from here? Can't I drop you off at your hotel?" she proposed.

"Thanks for the offer," I smiled at her, "but La Louisanne is more or less just round the corner, in the Rue de la Seine. In any case, I am in need of some exercise after all the extra calories I've consumed."

I withdrew my hand from her friendly clasp to offer it to her nephew.

"Good-bye, Jamie. I hope you find a suitable present for Nana. It was nice meeting you," I assured him, before taking my hand from his to offer it finally to Luke.

"Good-bye, Luke," I was very aware of the strength of his fingers as they took hold of mine. "I hope you enjoy the remainder of your holiday in Paris, and that you have no more similar disasters at the Luxembourg pond."

"Good-bye, Lisa," he continued to hold my hand as he spoke. "Thank you for being the right person at the right spot at the right time," his blue eyes held my gaze. "I hope all the photographs you take will turn out well, and that your novel travel guide will be a success. I wish you luck in future, although," the pressure on my fingers seemed to increase, "I expect your chestnut leaf will bring you all the good fortune you wish for."

Marguerite shot him a curious glance not understanding the allusion, and her frown deepened, when showing no hurry to depart, her brother continued to hold my hand and added.

"Thanks again for coming to our rescue to-day, Lisa. Jamie and I are indebted to you."

"Luke, you are embarrassing Lisa," Marguerite's tone was itself embarrassed. "She is in a hurry to get away, as you should be, if you don't want the sharp edge of Frédérique's tongue. You are in her black books as it is."

She took him firmly by the arm, and after another round of farewells they took off in the direction of the street where the Alfa was parked, uncle and aunt holding the hands of the boy who walked between them, looking down at him and laughing at something he had said to them, the picture of a happy family which gave me an untoward stab of envy.

I turned abruptly to walk off in the opposite direction, my sudden movement making me bump, painfully jarring my elbow, against a man who had come hurrying out of the brasserie. The encounter almost knocked us both off balance, but before I could recover my breath to apologise, the man uttered a vulgar French oath and not even glancing at me to see if I was all right, he went striding off in great haste, a man who had either over extended his luncheon break and was in fear of a reprimand from his employer, or perhaps an ardent lover on his way to his mistress, although how any woman could fancy such a vicious looking, foul mouthed character I couldn't understand.

That afternoon, try as I might, I couldn't help thinking about Luke and his nephew, wondering how they were getting on with their shopping, wondering, too, about the Frédérique Marguerite had mentioned so frequently. Was she young or old? Another sister? A friend of Marguerite or of Luke?

I even dreamed of Luke that night, and it was such a pleasant dream, I did not want to wake up when my travelling alarm told me it was time to rise.

He was still in my thoughts when I went to take a shower, and the more I thought about him, the more the man appealed to me. Although he had shown a helplessness in the face of Jamie's hysterical cries for his mother, I was certain he was a man who was usually in control of a situation:

44

a determined man, as his jaw line indicated; a man who liked to get his own way as he had shown when, having made up his mind to ask me to lunch, he had used all of his charm to make me say 'yes' when he had guessed at my hesitation.

He was also, I felt sure, a man who would do what he had set out to do and do it well. His command of French, when he had discussed the menu and wine list with the waiter at the brasserie had been so fluent he could have been taken for a Frenchman. He might be a hard man in business, whatever that business was, but he had his tender side, as I had seen in his dealings with Jamie.

I would have liked to have had the opportunity to have got to know him and count him among my friends.

I was still in the shower when the telephone in the bedroom buzzed. Frowning, I turned off the tap, hastily draped myself in the enormous bath towel which hung over the rail, and pushing my damp hair back from my forehead, I crossed the room to the bedside table, my feet leaving damp prints on the pile of the carpet.

"Who is speaking?" My response was automatically in English.

"Lisa, is that you?"

I decided that it was because I had been thinking of him that the voice I heard sounded like Luke's, for why should he, or anyone else for that matter, be telephoning me before eight in the morning.

"Yes. Lisa speaking," I spoke slowly.

"And this is Luke speaking," there was a lilt of laughter in the voice at the other end of the wire. "I hope my call didn't waken you. I know it is still quite early, but I did want to get in touch with you before you went out for the day."

"Is something wrong?" I asked anxiously. "And — and how did you know where to get in touch with me?"

"There is nothing wrong," he hastened

to assure me, "and if you remember, you mentioned the name of the hotel where you were staying when Marguerite offered to take you there."

"So I did," my tone was still questioning, for I couldn't think why Luke should be wanting to get in touch.

"It was just as well you did," he continued. "I forgot to return your scarf to you. I found it in my pocket last night, wondered what to do, and then Marguerite told me the name of your hotel. I was 'phoning to check that you would be in when we called round to give it to you."

I was going to see Luke again. It was unbelievable and wonderful. I grinned inanely at the mouthpiece.

"It's all right to come to the hotel, isn't it?" Luke sounded quite anxious. "You weren't going to go out right away?"

"Of course it's all right to come here," my voice lilted. "As for going out right away, I'm not dressed yet. I was having a shower when you telephoned. In any case, I also still have to have breakfast."

"That's good," Luke replied, then said, "Hold on a minute please, will you?"

I heard the murmur of voices faintly over the 'phone and then Luke spoke again.

"That was Jamie, asking if he could have a second breakfast with you? He is a demon when it comes to croissants. They are his favourite diet, even though he can't pile home-made cherry jam on top of them here as he does at home."

"Of course he can have a second breakfast with me," I answered cheerfully. "It's not often I have the opportunity to take my first meal of the day with a handsome young man, tell him that."

"With two handsome young men," Luke amended. "I'll be there too, remember? So cheers for now, Lisa. We should be with you by nine o'clock."

"Cheers!" I let out a happy breath as I replaced the receiver on its cradle, and towelling dry the wet patches on my body which the soft cotton hadn't yet absorbed from my skin during the conversation, I padded back to the bathroom where I dusted myself liberally with fragrant smelling talcum.

I buttoned up the cream and caramel striped shirt which I had decided to wear with my honey coloured cord trouser suit, tucked it in at the waistband, and sat down at the dressing table to put on some make-up.

I studied my reflection critically. Unlike Marguerite's, mine was not the kind of face that would attract a second glance. I had my mother's blue-grey eyes and barley coloured hair. I had inherited too, her neat features and fair complexion, but there was nothing outstanding about me. Nothing which could possibly hold the attention of a man like Luke.

From their manner, the expensive elegance of their clothes, a certain 'je ne sais quoi' about them, I had deduced that the Fletchers belonged to a world which was more sophisticated than my professional middle-class one. A world where the women would be in the same stylish mould as Luke's sister, and whose clothes would bear the label of an haute couture house instead of the label of the High Street store where I bought most of my clothes.

I picked up my tan leather shoulder bag, made sure I had an extra reel of film and my notebook inside, slung my camera case round my neck, and made my way to the lift.

When I stepped out into the reception hall I was greeted by a cry of "There she is", and Jamie came towards me as fast as his limping gait would let him, to make the very French gesture of shaking my hand to say 'Good morning'.

"You are in good time," I smiled at him. "Your uncle didn't think you would manage to get here until nine o'clock."

I took the hand Luke had extended

to me and said, smiling. "You must have ignored all the traffic lights to get here so quickly."

"We didn't come by car. I left it for Marguerite to use and took the Metro. Jamie likes travelling by Underground. It's a novelty."

"Rather him than me," I shivered slightly. "I only use it in cases of dire necessity. I get claustrophobic if I am underground for any length of time, so if I'm not walking, I prefer to make use of buses to get where I want to go in Paris."

I led the way to the breakfast room, where Jamie's appetite belied the slightness of his body. Luke had settled for only a cup of coffee, and watched with amusement as his nephew and I enjoyed a hearty breakfast.

"Where are you bound for to-day, Lisa?" he asked as I was wiping the stickiness from the cherry jam from my fingers. "I expect you will already have arranged to meet friends?" he spoke tentatively.

I shook my head. "I didn't manage to take any more photographs yesterday, because of the weather, and I'm getting behind the schedule I set myself so to-day, with the sun shining again, I must make up for lost time. There are streets near the Musée Carnavalet with very romantic histories which I would like to include in my book."

"The Musée Carnavalet?" Luke seized on the name. "That's a place I remember visiting when I was about Jamie's age. Oddly, I still remember it quite clearly, especially," he shook his head, "the guillotine scenes."

"You know," he spoke musingly, "I think Jamie would enjoy a visit there. Don't you?"

I would be a fool if I didn't guess that he was angling for an invitation to come with me, and although my pulses raced at the thought of spending another few hours with him, I sensibly told myself that it wasn't so much for my sake as for his own, that he was hoping I would take up the suggestion.

He was finding it difficult to entertain his nephew for hours on end, and remembering how well Jamie and I had got on the previous day, he was hoping that I would help him out.

"I'm sure he would," I said casually. "It is a very popular place for local school children to visit. St. Paul is the nearest Metro station, I believe."

He looked at me. "Lisa, would it be asking too much of you on our short acquaintance, if we came with you? Would it interfere with your work?"

Two pairs of eyes regarded me hopefully. Even if I had intended to refuse, I doubt if I could have withstood the joint appeal. However, I pretended to think it over before finally giving a nod of agreement, and saying.

"There would be a condition. If I should need a model to give a photograph more appeal, could I make use of Jamie?"

Jamie's smile of delight as he too rose to his feet was answer enough, and delight was a word I was to associate with the greater part of that day.

Because there wasn't a convenient bus route, because it was plain that Jamie with his limp wouldn't be able to walk great distances, I forced myself to propose that we should travel by Metro, and fortunately Jamie's constant chatter kept my mind occupied and I didn't have my usual feeling that the streets above the underground were going to cave in on us.

When we got out at St. Paul, we didn't make directly for the museum but went into a nearby Patisserie to buy three large and very creamy cakes which we ate on a bench in the tree-shaded Place des Voges. A small boy who was watching us ran up to Jamie and asked if he could play.

I didn't think Jamie would know what was being said to him, but to my astonishment he answered unhesitatingly in French, and still speaking that language, he came to his uncle to ask him if he could have his baton.

Luke handed it to him and stood for

a few moments to watch the youngsters having a mock duel. Then he turned to smile at me, but the smile changed to one of query.

"What's wrong, Lisa? Don't you approve?"

"Jamie speaks fluent French!" I exclaimed. "It's amazing."

"Why?" Luke appeared to be puzzled for a moment. "It is his father's language. But of course," realisation dawned, "you didn't know that, did you?"

"How could I? We are only casual acquaintances. Strangers until yesterday."

"Weren't you interested enough about us to ask a few questions?" He gave me a questioning look.

"Your sister didn't give me much opportunity to ask questions, and then with the talk of family skeletons I felt I had been wise not to show curiosity."

"There aren't really family skeletons, only family problems which are upsetting her very much at the moment. Let me explain about us."

"There's no need."

"I think there is. You will understand Jamie's reactions better if you know something of his background.

"Jamie is half French, as Marguerite and I are," he surprised me with this statement.

"Yes," he smiled at my expression, "we are all three hybrids. Our home is in St. Cécile in Dauphiny. My father was English, a visiting Professor at the University of Grenoble where my mother was a student. She was a de la Haie, like Jamie. When she married, her father gave her as a wedding present a villa on the family estate, on the understanding that she and her husband should settle there. My father, who was writing a history of the region, which he loved, was more than happy to accept this condition, but he made one proviso. Any of the children of the union should be born in England and brought up as English. You will see from this that my father could be as strong willed as the Count whose daughter he married."

"So that is why you and Marguerite talk English all the time."

"Not all the time. When we are en famille, yes. Otherwise we speak French. After all, we live in a French village. I work in the de la Haie family business where few of the staff speak any language but French, and my Uncle Henri, mother's brother, with whom we went to live after our parents were killed in a cable car accident, insisted we speak French to him. Uncle Henri was head of the family and liked to get his own way, sometimes deviously, although he did allow us to finish our education in England until we were both eighteen."

"Where does Jamie fit in?"

"I'm coming to that. One of the reasons Henri wanted Marguerite and me to live with him was that we would be company for his son, whose mother had died in the same accident as our parents, during holidays.

"Alain was a couple of years my senior, but we all got on very well together, and the bond between us became closer when his father remarried when Alain was seventeen.

"Some years later Alain himself married an English girl he had met while on a ski-ing holiday. To please her, he too made it a rule to speak English at home, much to the annoyance of his father and his step-mother, who couldn't speak a word of the language. Sometimes," Luke shook his head, "I felt certain that Alain insisted on the English speaking rule as much to annoy Giselle, whom he disliked, as to please his wife.

"However that is something which won't interest you. What I will tell you is that the Count died a year ago, and Alain inherited the castle, which put him in a position to carry out certain changes he had mooted to his father, but which Giselle, his step-mother, disapproved of. Six months ago, when he was driving Jamie down the steep and twisting road from the Château des Neiges to St. Cécile to call on a friend, a tyre blew out. In spite of Alain's efforts to control the subsequent spin, the car skidded across the road and toppled into the deep ravine on the left side."

I gasped with horror. "Oh, no!"

Luke hurried on, wishing the tale to be told before Jamie tired of the game he was playing and returned to our side.

"By some miracle Jamie was flung clear and escaped with bruising and a broken leg. You will notice he still limps, and he still is terrified of hurting it again.

"His mother was killed instantly, but Alain survived for a fortnight. Long enough to put his affairs in order. He wanted to make sure his plans for the castle would be carried out without interference from Giselle. He also nominated Marguerite and myself to be Jamie's guardians until he came of age, with the proviso that if Marguerite should marry before I did, she and her husband would take full responsibility for him, and make their home in the Castle. Similarly, if I married first, these terms applied to me. Alain wanted Jamie to be a member of a family unit, you understand."

I nodded. "He was lucky that you and your sister were so fond of him, and he knew he could rely on you."

"We weren't so lucky," retorted Luke grimly. "We didn't realise the complications there would be. When Marguerite's fiancé heard of the terms, he refused point blank to comply. His home is in Paris, his work is in Paris. Why should he give up everything, and take on a ready made family to boot? He has told Marguerite such a promise as she gave isn't binding, but like me," he spoke briskly, "she would not go back on her word. It's stalemate all round at the moment, with everyone concerned wanting to have things their own way."

"Does Jamie know what's going

on? Children are very sensitive to atmosphere. Poor little lad."

"Poor Marguerite," retorted Luke. "She is the one who is suffering at the moment. She has had to postpone the wedding which has caused a lot of talk, because no one knows the reason. I wish I could help her."

"You could, if you got married yourself," I pointed out. "It wouldn't be so difficult for you, would it? You live at the castle already. You work in St. Cécile. You are very fond of Jamie, anyone can see that."

Luke shot me a mocking glance.

"You make it sound quite simple, Lisa. You have forgotten one thing, though. I would have to find a woman who would be prepared to accept Jamie as well as me. As far as that is concerned, I have the same problem as Marguerite. But let's forget my family's worries for to-day. They don't concern you."

Jamie's playfellow had been called by his mother to come away as it was lunchtime, and Jamie returned to join us.

We enjoyed lunch in a pleasant restaurant in the Rue de Sévigné. We enjoyed our visit to the museum, where the miniature guillotines captured Jamie's fancy as they had captured his uncle's when he had been a boy, and we were lucky enough to see a cat prowling among the bushes outside a little tea room in the Rue des Barres.

Jamie's day reached its climax when the cat let him stroke it and I was able to take a photograph of it begging for food from his hand.

As we made our way to the nearest Métro station I told him I would send him copies of the photographs I had taken of him that day.

"You will have to tell me what address to post them to," I said.

Jamie glanced at his uncle, who replied for him.

"We are staying at a friend's house on the Ile St. Louis during our visit to Paris. I shall write the address down for you when we get on the Metro."

"I won't be getting the films developed until I return to Edinburgh. I shall need Jamie's home address."

"Couldn't you get them developed here?" pleaded Luke. "That way you could give them to Jamie in person and we could admire them together. You did say you would be in Paris for another ten days, didn't you?"

"You could take more photographs of me tomorrow," Jamie had no inhibitions. "I like being photographed. You make me do such funny things."

"Jamie, you mustn't take Lisa's company for granted. In any case," he eyed me quizzically, "I don't suppose you could put up with us for another day?"

My heart turned a somersault and I couldn't keep the glow of delight from my eyes. I knew perfectly well it was because I could help him entertain Jamie that Luke had suggested another meeting, yet I knew too that I had enjoyed this day more than any day for a long time, because I had spent it with this man who attracted me so very much.

"If you can put up with being trailed round odd streets, and if Jamie doesn't mind helping me out by looking for unusual sights for me, I don't mind at all if you join me. In fact, you are both helping me to see Paris with fresh eyes."

"Good. We'll call for you at the same time, shall we?"

I nodded, saying with a smile, "Shall I order breakfast for you again, Jamie?" while holding out my hand to say good-bye.

"Aren't you coming in the Métro with us?" asked Luke. "We'll be taking the same line."

"I was going to walk back to my hotel."

"From here? You will be exhausted. Come with us," he coaxed. "Your station is the one after ours. I'll hold your hand until then if you are nervous," he teased me in much the same way as I had heard him tease his sister.

He was right. It would be a long walk from here across to the other side of the river and the Rue de la Seine. It made sense to take the underground, yet I was still reluctant to do so.

Jamie took hold of my hand. "I'll look after you," he said gravely, tugging me towards the entrance to the station. "Come along."

In spite of Jamie's re-assurance I still felt nervous as we left street level, and when we had to change trains at the busy Châtelet station my nervousness increased. Perhaps it was the contrast between the quiet streets we had frequented during the day and the hustle and bustle and jostling of the evening crowds which made me feel so tense, but while we waited for our train to arrive, I was overwhelmed with such a feeling of fear, that when it came roaring towards us, still holding Jamie's hand, I turned and pulled him towards the exit.

As I did so, I was vaguely conscious of a movement close to me, and a man, who had been standing a foot or so behind me dashed forward, brushing my arm as I turned away, pushing viciously into the space I had vacated with such impetus that he couldn't stop himself in time and to the horror of those near to him he went plunging off the platform.

3

"**W**HAT'S happening? What's the man screaming for?" Jamie stopped in his tracks and tried to turn round and look back, but having had a horrified glimpse of what had happened from the side of my eye, I pulled the boy close to my side, holding his head against me, hands over his ears, to muffle them against the excited voice of a woman who had been standing near us.

"It was suicide," she gasped, while others on the platform surged past us to see what was going on. "He rushed forward, pushing me aside. If a woman and a little boy who had been standing in front of me hadn't happened to move away as he dashed forward, he would have taken them over the edge with him."

I waited to hear no more. I didn't want

Jamie involved in another nightmare, so grabbing his hand once more I pulled him against the tide of people and made for the exit, feeling quite shaken by what had taken place so close to us.

Suicide. What a way to take one's life. The momentary glimpse I had had of the man's face as he brushed violently against me still lingered for there was something about it which had caught my attention. I have a photographic memory, and I could have sworn I had seen that face before, but for the moment I couldn't recall where, nor did I want to. I wanted to erase totally from my mind the viciously contorted features and the awful scream he had uttered as he had plunged in front of the train.

Luke who had been standing a couple of feet away from me when my overwhelming feeling of claustrophobia had made me turn on my heel had become separated from us by the excited rubber-neckers, but I didn't wait for him to join us. I was too desperate to get away from the underground and gulp down some fresh air.

I was almost at the exit when I felt my arm grabbed and Luke said in a voice too low for Jamie to hear.

"Thank goodness you had the good sense not to stop back there. If Jamie had been involved as a witness to what happened, it would have revived memories of his own terrible accident, just when they were beginning to fade a little.

"What made you move away from me?" he continued, loud enough for Jamie to hear. "One minute you were standing beside me, next minute you were dashing away."

I gave a deprecatory laugh. "Would you believe it, I came over all funny, as they say. I did tell you I have a dislike of underground travel, and quite suddenly the feeling of claustrophobia got the better of me and I just had to get above ground."

"Thank God for your funny turn,"

69

Luke spoke softly again. "Do you realise that that madman would have knocked you under the train with him if you hadn't stepped aside when you did? Now, let's get away from here as quickly as possible. We don't want to be detained as possible witnesses," he indicated the uniform policemen who were hurrying down the long tunnel towards the platform we had left seconds earlier. "They will have plenty without us."

"Lulu, what are all those policemen doing here?" Again Jamie tried to glance back, but Luke had taken his other hand and was urging him firmly forward.

"Lisa's feeling a bit faint," he ignored the question. "We must get her into the fresh air as quickly as possible."

Jamie looked at me. "You do look funny," he agreed. "Your face has gone all white, like snow. Did you get a fright because that man gave such a funny scream?"

"I'm feeling faint because it is so

stuffy down here and because I hate being crowded in by lots of people, as we were back at the platform."

"I don't like a lot of people around me either," he replied. "That's why I don't like going shopping in Paris."

When we reached street level, Luke glanced around.

"We should be able to find a taxi. There is a rank nearby. It can drop Jamie and me off at the Ile St. Louis and then take you on to the left bank and your hotel."

"I'll walk," I shook my head. "I want to keep out in the air."

He studied my face. "No, Lisa. It will only take us minutes to get to our apartment. I will not leave you to walk back on your own, my dear. You will come with us, and have a brandy to bring a little colour back to your cheeks. You've had quite a shock, you know."

I didn't argue. My legs were feeling weak and would not have carried me far, I now realized. In any case, I didn't want to be on my own just yet. The face of the suicide still haunted me, and I didn't want it to. Another half hour with Luke and Jamie might help to dissolve the memory.

"Very well," I agreed. "I do feel weak about the knees still."

"You will be all right tomorrow, won't you?" Jamie's voice piped anxiously. "Luke was going to take me to the top of the Eiffel Tower, and I would like you to come with us. You would be able to get some lovely photographs," he coaxed.

"That's enough, Jamie," said Luke quickly. "We can't expect Lisa to give up any more of her time to us. She has gone out of her way to entertain us to-day, making the history of old Paris come alive for us in a way we won't forget," he turned to me with a smile. "We are both very grateful to you, Lisa."

Luke let go of my arm to hail a taxi, which swerved alongside us with a squeal of brakes.

"In you go, Jamie," he pushed the little boy inside. "Now you, Lisa," he helped me to climb in beside Jamie, following me quickly almost as though he was afraid I would change my mind about accompanying them and was determined not to let me have an opportunity to retreat from the cab.

He squeezed into the seat beside me, for small though Jamie was, there wasn't much room for three on the bench seat and we were packed so close that I could feel the pressure of Luke's leg against mine, of his hip against mine, and when, to give us a little more space he moved his arm from his side to lay it along the back of the seat, his fingers brushed casually against the nape of my neck, like a gentle caress. Their touch roused in me a sensation I had not known before. A thrill of delight and pleasure feathered through my veins. It was the kind of pleasure a lover's caress would give. I blushed at the thought and turned quickly from Luke, hoping he wouldn't notice the colour which now stained my cheeks, for to a man of the world, as I judged him to be, a girl who blushed when he accidentally touched her would seem an oddity, and I didn't want him to think of me as a gauche ingenue.

The taxi driver drove with typical Parisian elan, weaving his way in and out of the lines of traffic, turning so sharply to get into lane for the bridge which led to the Ile St. Louis, that Jamie swayed against me and I in turn swayed against Luke. His arm moved from the back of the banquette and circled my shoulders, holding me firmly and turning to say to me with a teasing smile.

"Now you see why I insisted on your coming with us by taxi. I wouldn't have found an excuse to do this on the Métro, would I?"

This time he couldn't but help see my blush, and his eyes glinted.

"I thought this might be a good way to get your colour back, Lisa, chérie. You were looking so ghostlike I felt I had to do something about it."

His teasing tone made me relax, because it was kindly teasing, and although he made no attempt to remove his grip, for my part I made no attempt to move from the casual embrace, not so much because I didn't want to appear over coy, but because I liked being held like this by Luke. I liked, too, the way his fingers now lightly kneaded my shoulder, and I was quite disappointed when, all too soon, we arrived at the address he had given the taxi driver, and he withdrew his arm, to lean forward and check the amount on the meter.

I followed him from the cab and stood on the pavement while he paid the fare.

"I'm feeling quite all right now, Luke," I told him, shrugging away the arm he was about to link in mine. "I don't need to come up for the brandy you talked of. I'll be able to walk back to my hotel from here."

"Nonsense," he said firmly, "you

are coming with us. You still have a fragile look about you," he studied my face. "It's not to be wondered at. You saw what happened in the Métro. That kind of thing is not easy to erase from memory, and I don't want you to brood over it on your own. Come, let's follow Jamie," he nodded towards his nephew who had gone ahead of us to open the door which led into the apartment building. "A brandy, or even just a cup of tea, is what you need at the moment. That, and the company of friends."

He urged me forward. "You know, I'm in your debt again, Lisa. If you hadn't made sure that Jamie couldn't see what was going on, he could have become hysterical. Any kind of accident has upset him badly since the car crash which killed his parents. He is only now getting over nightmares about that."

He looked down at me. "Lisa, I am beginning to think you have been appointed one of Jamie's guardian angels."

"First I am Florence Nightingale, now I'm a guardian angel," I tried to joke in an effort to pull myself together. "I wonder what role you will cast me in next?"

He shot me an appraising glance. "I'll think of something. How about courtesy aunt?"

Jamie, who was trying to stifle a yawn as we approached the door he was holding open heard this.

"You would have to marry Lisa to make her my aunt, wouldn't you, just like Marguerite has to marry Edouard to make him another uncle?"

Luke laughed. "I'll bet you would like that, young man. You would like to have Lisa around all the time to keep you amused, wouldn't you?"

Jamie nodded. "Yes, so will you marry her, Lulu?"

My cheeks may have been snow white earlier, now they were rose red with embarrassment, and seeing my confusion Luke said sternly.

"That's enough, Jamie. You've upset Lisa."

Jamie's shoulders drooped, as much with weariness as with dismay at his uncle's unexpectedly sharp tone and I felt sorry for him. I put my hand into his and gave his fingers a squeeze.

"Your uncle has probably someone else in mind to marry, Jamie, so she would be your aunt, but I could still be a courtesy aunt, which means an aunt specially chosen to be a friend. Shall we settle for that?"

"Yes, please," he snuggled into my side and over his head I encountered a smile of relief from Luke, pleased at the way I had handled the situation.

When we reached the flat Marguerite opened the door.

"We have had a long and exciting day," Luke explained. "I've invited Lisa here for a drink to revive her before she returns to her hotel. Believe me," he glanced at me with a smile, "she is in need of a pick-me-up."

He stepped past his sister into the little hall. "Jamie is already almost out for the count, so I suggest you get him ready for bed while I pour the drinks."

Jamie, in the way that children do, had suddenly come to life again and struggled from his uncle's arms.

"We had a great day, Marguerite. We saw a guillotine, you know the thing that used to chop people's heads off, and we had sword fights in the park and we saw a cat . . . "

"You can tell me all about it while you get ready for bed and I prepare your supper," said Marguerite firmly, adding in a more bitter tone. "I can't say the same for myself. Frédérique kept on at me to-day, much as Edouard did yesterday, telling me what I ought to do. Neither of them seem to realise how difficult things are for me. They think only of themselves."

Pouting, she led Jamie away, while Luke ushered me into the lounge, where he crossed to the cocktail to get three brandy glasses, into which he poured a fine Napoleon brandy.

"Poor Marguerite," he shook his head as he came to where I was standing to hand me a glass. "She is finding life very hard at the moment. I hate seeing her so upset. If only she and Edouard had been married before Alain had extracted that promise from us when he was dying, things would have been so different. It has been very difficult for all concerned."

"Poor Jamie," I said, cradling the brandy glass in my hand. "He is a bright lad. He must be aware of what's going on."

"No. We've kept the conditions from him, although there are times when Marguerite comes close to making a faux pas.

"You have a soft spot for my nephew, don't you, Lisa?" he asked me unexpectedly.

"He is a charmer," I said, refraining from adding that in this respect he took after his uncle. "He's full of life and mischief, yet he is affectionate, too. I doubt if any woman will be able to resist him when he gets older."

"Frédérique seems immune to his charm," said Marguerite who had re-entered the room in time to hear the tail end of our conversation. "She would find him even less attractive if she could see him at this moment splashing about in the bath and getting soap and water all over the place."

"Frederique isn't used to children," Luke made excuses for the absent woman. "Being the only child of elderly parents, and having no cousins, or nephews or nieces for that matter, she can't understand them."

"She was a child herself," I put in rather tartly. "You've only to cast your mind back to the things you did when you were young to have some understanding. Not," I sighed, "that understanding always makes for patience when a child is trying to exert his personality. Battles of wills can be difficult."

"Not just with children," Marguerite

grimaced, hastily turning to dash from the room as a particularly noisy splash followed by a yell emanated from the bathroom at the end of the corridor.

"That's Jamie exercising his personality," Luke grinned at me.

I smiled back at him, and as we continued to look at each other, I was more than ever aware of the very strong attraction this man, who had been a stranger less than forty-eight hours ago, had for me.

Because I didn't want him even to guess how much he charmed me, I looked away from him, and raised the glass of brandy to my lips.

Jamie, in a pair of sky blue pajamas, his damp hair curling round his head and giving him the look of a Botticelli angel, came into the room, followed by Marguerite.

"Jamie has come to say goodnight, and also to ask you a special question, Lisa," she glanced across at me.

"What is it you want to know?" I asked Jamie.

"You know I told you we were going to the Eiffel Tower tomorrow, but you didn't say if you would come with us or not, so I'm asking you again. You will come, won't you?" he pleaded.

"Jamie!" exclaimed Marguerite. "That's enough. Lisa has been very kind, giving up one of her days to you, but you can't expect her to spend any more of her holiday time with you. She will have her own plans. She will want to go out with her own friends."

"But I am her friend," said Jamie. "She told me so. She said she would be a kind of aunt who is a special friend, didn't you?" he appealed to me for confirmation. "So if I'm your friend, we can go together tomorrow, can't we?"

"You are a little monkey," I bent down and gave him a quick hug. "You are trying to appeal to the softness of my heart, aren't you?"

"Of course he is," frowned Marguerite. "He's used to getting his own way since — " she stopped and amended what she had been about to say by adding lightly. "Already he seems to have his uncle's way with women."

A warning bell sounded in my head. Marguerite had spoken casually enough, yet at the same time she had given me the impression that she was none too happy about the effect I was having on Jamie and even less happy about the fact that her brother had seemed to enjoy meandering around Paris with a stranger, and had made no demur when Jamie had proposed another day in my company. The hint that Luke was something of a ladies' man had been made deliberately, to warn me off.

If Luke himself read anything into her words, he ignored it, smiled across at me and said.

"That just goes to show that like me where women are concerned, Jamie has excellent taste. All the same," he continued more seriously, "don't let our young nephew coerce you into doing something you don't want to

84

do, Lisa. If you have had your fill of our company, I'll understand if you refuse, although," his eyes, blue as the tall delphiniums in the crystal vase on the table beside him, looked directly into mine, asking, not pleading, as his nephew's glance had done, "I would be delighted if you were free to help me keep Jamie out of mischief for another day."

He gave his sister a look which warned her not to interfere. "Marguerite is so tied up with her own affairs just now she hasn't time to come with us."

"Please say yes, Lisa," Jamie, unaware of the tension between brother and sister, looked at me with his pansy dark eyes.

I should have said 'No' straightway. But I was going to say yes. But I must phrase my acceptance in such a way that it would appear I was doing so to please Jamie; so that Marguerite, who was looking at me as if she was willing me to say 'No' would not guess at my feelings for her brother. My feelings were private. I would keep them so. It was with a glance at Jamie, and in a tone which was light and casual I replied.

"As a matter of fact, you will be doing me a favour by letting me come with you, Jamie. You see," I explained, my attention directed to Marguerite rather than her brother. "To-day's outing has given me a totally new perspective of Paris. To-day I saw the city not as a place I know well, but through the eyes of a child, to whom everything was fresh and new. Things intrigued him which I had overlooked. Now I have a new concept for my book. There is Jamie's Paris, of unusual street names, and of the fun of joining with the boys who played at marbles in the street. There is my Paris, of flower filled parks and old men playing boules on the gritty ground.

"Tomorrow, I am quite sure Jamie will draw my attention to other people and places I might have overlooked."

Jamie didn't let me say any more.

"Does that mean you are going to come with us?" he beamed.

I nodded.

He darted from his aunt's side to come and put an arm round me, damp hair pressed against my waist as he exclaimed in delight. "That's great. Lisa, I do love you!"

Even Marguerite had to give a reluctant smile at his enthusiastic thanks.

"These are dangerous words to say to a woman, Jamie," Luke was smiling too. "In fact, you should never say them unless you really mean them," he teased.

"I hope you follow your own advice," Marguerite challenged him.

"But of course," his voice was bland.

Marguerite said quickly, "Jamie, your supper will be getting cold. Off you go and eat it, then brush your teeth before you go to bed. I shall come and tuck you in later, after Lisa has gone. Say 'Goodnight' to her now."

Jamie detached himself from me to

shake me solemnly by the hand. "A demain, Lisa," he said, nothing solemn in the happy look he gave me as he scampered off to do Marguerite's bidding.

When he had gone I said. "I must be on my way, too.

"Won't you join us for a meal?" Marguerite suggested politely.

I resisted the temptation. "No thanks. I must get back to the hotel. I want to write up my impressions of what we did to-day while they are still fresh in my memory."

"Where shall we meet tomorrow, Lisa?" asked Luke. "Shall I call for you at the hotel?"

"There is no need for that. As we are going to the Tour Eiffel I suggest we meet on the south side, where the lifts are, at ten o'clock. That is when the doors open."

"I'll be there," he smiled. "Being gentlemen," he cast a sly glance at his sister, "we won't keep you waiting."

I moved towards the door, but Luke

detained me. "I've an idea you intend to walk back, but I don't think you should. I'll 'phone for a taxi."

"There is no need to do that. I shall get a bus near the Pont Marie."

"Nonsense," Luke brushed aside the suggestion. "I would have driven you back myself, but we are expecting friends for dinner in about half an hour. That's why Marguerite invited you to stay and dine with us," he smiled across at his sister. "She knew there was a meal already prepared and an extra guest would make no difference. Are you sure you won't change your mind and join us?"

"Thanks, Luke, but I must get back."

"In that case, I shall 'phone for a taxi, and no arguments," he spoke firmly.

"You had better give in gracefully, Lisa," Marguerite's smile was friendlier. "I must say I agree with him, for once. You look tired, which isn't surprising after spending a whole day with Jamie!"

When the cab drove up Luke took my hand. "Goodbye, Lisa. Thanks for a pleasant day and for being so kind to Jamie."

He raised my hand to his lips in a gallant gesture. "Safe home, my dear."

With that he helped me into the taxi and stood on the narrow pavement, to give a final wave of his hand when the cab turned the corner out of his view.

His friendly gesture, the knowledge that I would be seeing him again tomorrow made me light-headed as well as light-hearted.

I dreamed of him that night, then woke up, to scold myself for having such strong feelings for a man who was still virtually a stranger. The coming day would be a failure.

It wasn't. Nor were the following days when Luke, learning that the friends I had intended to visit when in Paris were on holiday and that I would be wandering round the city on my own, insisted that I joined Jamie and him for their daily excursions. In this way, I was able to do things and see things I had not thought of before. By the end of ten days together I knew I was falling in love with Luke. I knew, too, how foolish this was, for tomorrow, and this I could hardly believe because the days had passed so quickly, I would be going home. This afternoon, when I said goodbye to Luke and Jamie it would be a final goodbye.

Of course, I turned away so that Luke would not hear my sigh, we would exchange addresses so that I could send on to Jamie those photographs which would interest him, and we would say that we must keep in touch, but keeping in touch would only be the exchange of Christmas cards for a year or two, not a promise of continuing friendship.

Marguerite had made me subtly aware of differences between us when we had talked together. She had raised her eyebrows and glanced at Luke when I had told them that before going to work for my father I had taught English in a finishing school near Montreux, which turned out to be the finishing school her friend Frédérique, who was her partner in the firm of interior decorators which Marguerite herself had started, had attended.

"A penny for your thoughts?" Luke switched his attention from Jamie who had gone off to look at the mechanical pigeons which some young Algerians were trying to sell to strollers in the park.

"A penny?" I sighed.

"Are they worth more than that?"

"At to-day's rate of exchange, much more," I quipped, making an effort to be light-hearted.

"Shall I write a cheque for them?"

I half laughed, but there was a sob in my laughter. I was going to miss these amusing exchanges with Luke as much as I was going to miss just being with him.

"I was thinking that this time tomorrow I shall be on my way home," I told him.

Luke's astonishment made his voice rise.

"Lisa, I didn't know you were leaving Paris so soon. Lisa, you can't go off and leave us," he protested. "Jamie will be heartbroken. You've made this a wonderful holiday for him."

"I'll miss Jamie too," I looked across at the small boy.

"And me? Will you miss me, Lisa?"

The question was unexpected. It brought a betraying flush to my cheeks. I looked quickly away from him, back to Jamie, so that he wouldn't surprise the answer in my expressive eyes.

"You will, won't you?" he put his hand under my chin and turned my face so that I was forced to look at him.

"You will, won't you?" he repeated softly.

"Please, Luke, let me be." I tried to pull myself away, but his fingers were still tight on my jaw and I was unable to do so.

"You will, won't you?" he said the words again, very softly.

"You know I will," I admitted gruffly.

"Then why go? Why leave me?"

"My holiday is over. I have to get back to work. I have to earn my living, you know. In any case, father can't cope on his own much longer. He told me on the 'phone only last night that he has been inundated with orders for wedding photographs. November and December seem to be popular months with brides this year."

There was a long silence. Luke had taken his fingers from my chin, to rest his hand on my own one, which was nervously plucking at a miniscule piece of fluff on my skirt. When he spoke, his words were not words I had expected to hear.

"You could be a November or a December bride too, Lisa, if you married me," his grip on my hand tightened. "You wouldn't need to earn your living then," the usual teasing note crept into his voice. "I would be able to keep you in the luxury to which you are accustomed."

It was heartless of him to make a joke like this about love and marriage. To think I had believed him to be a kindly man. All he cared for was his own amusement.

I turned on him angrily.

"Marguerite was right to warn me about you. She told me last night that you couldn't resist flirting with a woman, any woman, but I didn't believe her. I told her we were just good friends, that you hadn't given me more than a courtesy kiss, and she laughed, not believing. But she was right," I glared at him. "Now you have spoilt everything."

"Have I?" he placed his hand back under my chin and made me look at him again, so that there was no way I could hide the tears which had come into my eyes. "Surely not? Surely you can't forget the pleasure we have found in each other's company? The shared laughter, the talk, our mutual fondness for young Jamie?"

His fingers moved from my chin to my neck, gently stroking my skin, now casually twisting the hair at the back of my head in a way which sent a pleasurable emotion feather up and down my spine, weakening my resolve to move away from him.

"Dear Lisa," his eyes, bluer than the cloudless autumn sky overhead held my gaze. "I'm not flirting with you. I don't want just a casual relationship with you. I want you to be my wife."

I was hypnotized by the effect of his caressing touch, unable to move, unable to find tongue to reply to him.

"Don't you want to marry me Lisa? Are you afraid to let your emotions get the better of you? Are you too much of a career woman, to give it up for love?"

Again his hand was cupped under my chin, and he looked at me as if probing to my very heart to find the answer, willing me to give the response he wanted rather than argue for it.

I still couldn't believe he was serious. Surely a man like Luke would want, as his sister had hinted, someone more sophisticated, more elegant than I was for his wife; someone from his own jet set circle of friends.

"Well?"

His eyes continued to hold my gaze, and looking into them I realised, with a growing sense of delight, that he was serious in his demand.

"Luke!" I found my voice at last. "You aren't just teasing me. I thought at first you were, because it's — it's so unbelievable, and" — words came out in a nervous jumble before I finally took a long, deep, steadying breath and with a nod of my head said slowly,

"Yes, Luke, I'll marry you, but oh," I gave a breathless laugh, "Pinch me, darling, so that I know I'm not dreaming."

He didn't pinch me. Instead, oblivious of the people strolling past, he kissed me long and hard on the lips, a kiss so very different from the casual goodnight kisses we had exchanged in the past days, a kiss so demanding, so urgent, it convinced me, had I still needed to be convinced, that I wasn't dreaming.

Luke only released me from his embrace when Jamie came running towards us, stopping on his way to snatch at a falling leaf. He missed it and his smile crumpled into a look of dismay.

"Does that mean I'll have bad luck?" he asked anxiously.

I put out my hand and drew him to me. "Catching falling leaves is just a game, nothing more."

Yet, I thought, catching my chestnut leaf had brought me wonderful luck. Hopefully Jamie's failure meant nothing. Of course it didn't, I assured myself, but my assurance was negated by a sudden chill in my bones which made me shiver; by the kind of pricking in my thumbs which my mother had once told me presaged something direful about to happen. I was being over fanciful because I was emotionally excited I tried to laugh away the premonition. Nothing direful could possibly happen to spoil this day for me.

I smiled at Jamie, and gently pushed his tousled hair back from his forehead.

"I don't know what you were going to wish for, Jamie, but your uncle has something to tell you which I think will make up for not catching your leaf. It's something very special."

4

JAMIE'S reaction to Luke's announcement was as excited and enthusiastic as we had expected it to be.

"That means you will be my real aunt, not the other kind, doesn't it? And it means too," he beamed from one to other of us, "that Lisa will be coming to live with us at the Château des Neiges for ever and ever. You won't be going back to Scotland and leaving us as Luke said you would soon be doing."

I smiled at my new fiancé over his nephew's shoulders.

"I must go home to Scotland, Jamie. In fact, I'm going there tomorrow, but it will only be for a short time, until your uncle and I marry. After that I shall come back to France with him, and we'll live in St. Cécile, for ever and ever," I repeated his words gaily.

I had known that Jamie's reaction to the engagement would pose no problems, but I suspected that neither Marguerite nor my father would greet the news with such whole-hearted delight.

When we returned to the flat on the Ile St. Louis, and Luke told his sister he had asked me to marry him, her jaw dropped and she gaped at him in astonishment. Then, regardless of my presence, in her usual impetuous way, she said the first thing which came into her mind.

"Luke, you're joking. You can't marry Lisa. Everyone expects you to marry — "

"Of course everyone expects me to marry," Luke interrupted her smoothly. "You and Nana have been on at me for long enough to settle down. Aren't you pleased I have taken your advice at last?"

She gaped at him not quite sure if she should take him seriously, then stammered, "B-but — "

101

"But aren't you going to congratulate us?" Luke asked, slipping his arm round my waist. "You will be making Lisa think you don't want her for a sister-in-law."

"I'm sorry. You took my breath away. It's so unexpected." She embraced her brother. "I do congratulate you," she murmured as Luke gently propelled her in my direction, "and you have my best wishes, Lisa," she kissed me lightly on both cheeks, but I sensed a reluctance in her tone and in her actions.

"We bought a bottle of champagne on our way here, to celebrate," Luke flourished the bottle, "so while you go and telephone Edouard to tell him the good news and ask him to come and join us, I'll go and put it on ice until he arrives."

He urged his sister from the lounge, firmly closing the door behind him, while I, somewhat shaky with excitement, helped Jamie off with his jacket and asked him to take it, with mine, to hang in the cloakroom by the front door.

I didn't mean to eavesdrop, but as he opened the door to go into the hall, I heard raised voices from the kitchen at the end of the short corridor.

"Luke, I feel dreadful," Marguerite's tone was troubled. "I didn't mean what I said last night. You surely knew that. There is no need for you to react the way you have done. Things will work out without causing a fresh lot of problems."

"Things are working out, my dear, so no more arguments and no misgivings. Now, off you go and telephone Edouard. Tell him my good news. You can also tell him another bottle of champagne won't go amiss, since we all have something to celebrate."

As Jamie returned to the lounge and closed the door, I wondered, vaguely, what Luke and Marguerite had been at loggerheads over, but almost instantly dismissed the problem. I wasn't going to let an argument between brother and sister which wasn't my concern, spoil this special day for me. I was in love. The man I loved had asked me to marry him. For the moment nothing else and no one else mattered.

Edouard's congratulations, when he arrived at the flat half an hour later were warm and sincere, but my father's reception of the news when I telephoned him later that evening was not over enthusiastic. I sensed his disapproval in his cautious words about hoping that I hadn't let myself be swept off my feet by a holiday romance which might not be the real thing, might be something I would later regret, but his doubts as to the wisdom of what I was doing could no more dampen my euphoria than Marguerite's equally unenthusiastic reception of the announcement had done.

I had hoped that I could have persuaded Luke to come to Scotland for the few days left of his holiday so that he could meet my father and set his mind at rest about his future son-in-law, but this had been impossible.

Both father and Marguerite thought

we were rushing things when Luke and I decided to be married before the end of the year, but I saw no reason for a long engagement. I loved Luke. I didn't want to be parted from him any longer than was necessary, and although Luke himself had never actually said to me, 'I love you, Lisa,' the brilliant three stone diamond ring on my engagement finger said the words for him.

There was so much to do to prepare for a wedding at such short notice, I hadn't time to pay any attention to my father's continued misgivings about the marriage. I was inclined to put them down to the fact he was upset because I would be making my home in a foreign land a thousand or so miles away from him. I felt sad about this too, but I consoled myself with the fact that my sister lived near to Edinburgh, and she and her children would be able to visit him often and cheer him up.

Christmas Day, falling as it did three days before the wedding day, turned out to be rather an emotional event. I had hoped Luke would come to Scotland in time for it, but Jamie wanted to spend this special day in his own home with his own family, and Luke felt obliged to fall in with the little boy's natural wishes. I could understand Jamie's feelings, but they did bring home to me very sharply that this time next year I would be spending Christmas Day in a foreign land, remote from my own family and friends, and this made me feel tearful.

However, the excitement of Luke's arrival on our wedding eve, the relief I felt when father told me that having met Luke, he no longer had doubts about my choice of husband, made me forget the sadness I had felt on Christmas day.

My wedding day couldn't have begun more perfectly. Sunshine shone on a world which had been transformed by a hard overnight frost into a winter wonderland.

My wedding dress was of white

velvet, simply cut, high necked, long sleeved, nipped in to emphasize my neat waist. My only jewellery would be the star-shaped diamond ear-rings, the gift of the groom, to match the magnificent engagement ring he had given me earlier. My bouquet would be a spray of snow white orchids with golden centres, tied with a golden bow into which father had tucked a spray of white heather for luck.

Marguerite's fiancé Edouard was to be best man, my sister Iona-Jane, matron-of-honour, and Jamie and my nephew Niall were to be pages.

As well as Marguerite, Edouard and Jamie, several of Luke's friends had flown to Scotland with him for the wedding. My father had invited them to dinner in the station hotel on the eve of the wedding so that he could meet them and tell them of the wedding arrangements, and my sister had been a trifle over-whelmed by the jet set elegance of the women.

Now, as my father and I were

standing in the entrance to the church, waiting for the organ to start the wedding march, he gave me a final piece of advice.

"Lisa, my dear. You must know that you are marrying into a different world from ours. Don't let it frighten you when the glamour of the wedding is over and you face the reality of day to day living. Don't alter your own values. Remember this, Luke chose you to be his wife because you are who you are, a sincere, down to earth young woman; a gingerbread girl without the gilt of high society."

"Gingerbread indeed!" I chaffed him. "I hope there is no big bad wolf in the offing waiting to swallow me up."

The church officer nodded to us to be ready. The music swelled triumphantly. I tucked my arm in my father's and slowly, serenely, walked down the aisle to the man I loved.

I was vaguely aware of my friends turning to smile at me, of the strangers who were Luke's friends staring at me with curiosity, then suddenly, startlingly, I became aware of one particular face, the face of the woman seated beside Marguerite. No doubt it was a trick of the light, or possibly the folds of my veil distorted the expression on her face, but she appeared to be looking at me with such malevolence that I was taken aback, and as I moved forward the final few feet to where Luke was standing I missed my step and stumbled.

Luke who had been waiting for me, smiling, immediately put out his hand to steady me. The warm clasp of his hand, the momentary caress of his fingers steadied me immediately and made me forget the flight of fancy which had made me imagine that the woman who had stared at me so intently wished me ill.

Later, when I was standing with my new husband in the hotel ballroom where the reception was being held, I found myself waiting with some apprehension to be introduced to this woman, but she didn't appear. I decided, with an overwhelming feeling of relief, that she hadn't after all, been a wedding guest, only one of those women who enjoy coming to church to watch every wedding they can, although why a casual spectator should have seated herself beside the groom's sister I couldn't imagine.

We had chosen Paris for our honeymoon. On the flight we toasted our future again with champagne, as we had earlier toasted it at the reception. We drank champagne too at our very first dinner together at Maxim's. I became light-headed with the wine which bubbled on my lips and tongue like teasing kisses. I was light-headed, too, with happiness, knowing that tonight our goodnight kisses would not be parting kisses.

So much champagne, so much happiness made me both dizzy and giggly, much to Luke's amusement, but there was more than amusement in his glance when he gazed down at me as he carried me across the threshold of the bridal suite of the hotel where we would spend a few days before going to St. Cécile-les-Lacs, the village in Dauphiny where I would be spending the rest of my life.

However, I did not think of the future that night, only of the present. I had not guessed that love-making would be so wonderful. Luke was a tender and considerate lover. When I wept with sheer emotion, he kissed my tears away with lips which were soft and gentle as the touch of a butterfly's wings.

Each night was more perfect than the last, just as each day we spent in Paris was more perfect than any other day. Paris had been a golden city in late October when we had first met. At the year's end it was a city of damp drizzle alternating with downpours of rain, which sent us splashing through puddles to seek shelter when we went to revisit our October haunts, but for me the sun still shone. I walked on golden clouds, not muddy streets.

I didn't want the honeymoon to end, yet on the morning that we were due to leave for St. Cécile, I woke up unusually early. I had had a disquieting dream, the first nightmare I had had for months.

However it wasn't the dream that troubled me, but the knowledge that to-day we would be leaving Paris, and I didn't want to. I didn't feel ready for St. Cécile and the new life I would have to make there, among strangers. What worried me most was that we were going to live for a few weeks in the Château des Neiges before moving into our own home which wasn't yet ready for us.

Luke had explained that he and Marguerite had their own wing in the Chateau, and it was there I would stay. Jamie and Nana lived in the main house, their rooms in the corridor which led to our wing, and the Countess de la Haie, Jamie's grandmother, occupied another wing.

The same staff served everyone and everyone met for the main meals in the dining room. The Countess and her son had not come to the wedding and I was nervous at meeting my future hostess for the first time.

I shivered again, and this time Luke opened his eyes and frowned at me.

"What's wrong, Lisa? You haven't caught a chill after yesterday's soaking?"

"No, I'm not cold, Luke. I'm just nervous. It's going to be strange for me, arriving at St. Cécile, making my home with people I haven't met yet, your aunt and cousin, even Nana. I've been lying awake thinking that the Countess may resent me coming to live in her home and that's why she didn't come to the wedding."

"Don't be silly, darling," he kissed the cold tip of my nose. "I explained why Giselle and Jean Claude couldn't come to Scotland. Jean Claude had an important ski race he didn't want to miss, and his mother wouldn't come without him. She dotes on him, as you will soon find out."

"Giselle is my late uncle's second wife. He married her three years after Alain's mother died, and as you can imagine, Alain was far from pleased when his father unexpectedly brought home as his step-mother a woman of twenty-seven, only ten years older than he was. He wasn't only angry, he was embarrassed, and he wasn't the only one," Luke's smile was malicious. "You see, my uncle was so besotted with Giselle he didn't want to lose her, so he hadn't mentioned he had a son, never mind an almost grown up son. He had met her in Cannes and he married her there, with none of his own family aware of the wedding."

"That wasn't fair, was it? The poor girl must have had quite a shock."

"Fair?" Luke seized on the word. "Don't they say all is fair in love and war and my uncle was in love, or rather was completely infatuated by Giselle and he didn't want to lose her. Not that she was the loser in any way.

Marriage to a very rich man with a title lifted her from playing minor parts in the theatre to playing the role of lady of the manor in St. Cécile and write ups in the social and not the variety columns."

"You don't like her, do you?" I looked at him with a surprised frown.

Luke's fingers stopped caressing me. He didn't answer immediately then eventually said thoughtfully.

"Giselle is all right, but I always feel she is acting a part, the part of a society woman, to hide her humbler origins and I like people to be themselves. You have nothing to worry about where she is concerned, Lisa. All you have to do is tell her her son is wonderful and keep Jamie from calling her grand'mère. She thinks it wrong that he should do so, because she isn't really his grandmother, but more importantly, it conveys the impression that she is a lot older than she is. Jean Claude is her only darling."

The flight to Grenoble was late in

taking off because of poor visibility, the journey was unpleasantly bumpy, and I was glad when we eventually touched down. Marguerite was meeting us with her car.

There were flurries of snow as we left the plane, and the mountains which encircled Grenoble were totally covered. I shivered, but not from physical cold, for the fur coat which Luke had bought me in Paris as an extra wedding present kept out the chill wind. It was deep inside that I felt cold. Cold with panic. Cold with a fear of the unknown, with a presentiment that my arrival at the Château des Neiges would not be welcomed by all the family.

Luke gave my arm an impatient tug.

"Come along, Lisa. It's much too cold to stand and stare." He took my arm and hurried me towards the airport building where, after a short delay we picked up our excess luggage.

Marguerite, looking like a Vogue advertisement for what the well dressed woman should wear for a winter holiday, came towards us, smiling. She gave Luke an affectionate hug, kissed me, French fashion on both cheeks and warned us that heavy falls of snow were forecast, so that we had better get on our way as quickly as possible.

She eyed our trolley-load of luggage with mock dismay.

"I should have brought the Mercedes to accommodate that lot," she shook her head.

"How is Jamie?" I asked. "I thought he might have come with you to meet us."

"He wanted to, but I said 'No'. In weather like this the car might skid a little, and I didn't want him to be frightened, and reminded of his accident."

She led the way to where she had parked her car. "He really is excited about your arrival, Lisa," she turned round to smile at me. "He is planning all sorts of things for you to do with him, and places he wants to show you."

Luke grinned as he helped me into the scarlet Alfa. "It would seem I am going to have a rival for your affections, Lisa," he teased. "Still, I don't mind. Being with Jamie will keep you out of mischief during the day when I am at work."

Luke told me the name of the villages we passed through, pointing out in one the paper factory which had been in the de la Haie family for generations, and where he would be working for another few weeks, until he began the task his cousin Alain had asked him to carry out for him, the conversion of the Château des Neiges from a too large, too expensive to run family house, into a luxury hotel and sports complex, which would be owned by Jamie as Alain's heir, but managed by Luke.

The road became narrower and steeper, with snow piled high at one side. Marguerite was driving with care, and I found myself gripping the edge of the seat, for at times we seemed only inches from the sheer drop into the gorge on our right. I didn't want Luke to think I was scared, but I couldn't help tensing my body when the wheels spun for a second on a lump of snow. Immediately he sensed my unease and put a hand gently on mine.

"Everyone finds this road a bit frightening at first, but believe me, you get used to it. What's more, it is less frightening when you are driving yourself than when you are being driven."

"If Jamie is ever in the car with you, Lisa," Marguerite warned me, "Take especial care at this corner. This is where his parents' car went over the edge, and he still panics a bit when he passes the spot if he thinks a car is being driven too fast."

She slowed down to negotiate a hairpin bend with sheer rock rising up on one side of the road, and an equally sheer rock face on the other side plunging down into the unseen gorge far below.

"It is a pity he has to pass this spot every time he leaves the Chateau, but there is no other road to St. Cécile."

I shook my head. "I don't think I shall have the nerve to drive on this road."

Luke slipped his arm round my shoulder. "Of course you will," he encouraged me. "This is the worst part, and it is perfectly safe if you take it at the correct speed. Alain's accident was caused by a tyre blowing out at this particular spot, and that was a chance in a million. In any case," he assured me, "I'll come with you until you feel confident about driving on your own."

Before he had finished speaking we had rounded the bend and now the road widened and turned away from the gorge. The rock faces receded and now on either side there were gentler slopes. On the right, the slope stretched up to an attractive looking chalet type house, sheltered on three sides by pine trees.

Luke nudged me.

"That is the Villa des Narcisses, Lisa," there was pride in his voice. "That is our future home. What do you think of it?"

"Oh!" I let out a long breath. "What an attractive house. What a wonderful view it must have."

For the first time since arriving in Dauphiny my feeling of nostalgia, my doubts that I might not settle happily so far from my native land, vanished. I couldn't take my eyes from the villa. I liked the style of the architecture, the steep sloping roofs, the verandahs, its setting among the trees with the glorious sweep of Alpine meadow going right down to the roadway. I could imagine how it must look in summer, its window boxes brilliant with geraniums, the stretch of meadow carpeted with the wild flowers for which the area was famous. I could imagine being happy in such a house, bringing up a family there.

I managed to tear my gaze away and turn to my husband to say with delight.

"Darling, it's a perfect house. I know we'll be happy there!"

He gave me a pleased grin. "I rather thought it would appeal to you."

As we drove on, the snow became heavier with alarming quickness. In minutes visibility was reduced to yards.

"Thank goodness we've made it in time," said Marguerite, turning the car into a gateway which was only just visible now. "Everyone is looking forward to meeting you especially Jean-Claude."

"He would," grimaced Luke. "Let me warn you, my dear, to watch out for that young man. He may be only seventeen, but he already fancies himself as a lady killer.

"There are no family ghosts to scare you either," he went on, with another reassuring pressure of his fingers. "They all went down the drains when my uncle installed new plumbing."

The car swept up the driveway and along the front of the building, where snow clung to the façade, overhung roofs and turrets and window ledges, so that if it hadn't been for the lights gleaming from the various windows, the long, high edifice would have been invisible in the whiteness of the blizzard. How aptly it had been named, I thought. Le Château des Neiges. The castle of the snows.

Within seconds of our arrival, a massive door was opened by an elderly man, who came hurrying down the steps to open the car doors.

Luke greeted the man then hustled me across the few feet of snow covered ground, up the slippery steps and into a rectangular hall. Marguerite followed right on our heels, carrying our overnight cases which had been dumped on the front seat of the Alfa.

"Take Lisa up to your suite right away, Luke," she advised as we stamped the snow from our feet. "She must be longing to freshen herself and take a few deep breaths before meeting the family. Maurice will take the rest of the luggage up, while I go and tell Giselle you have arrived."

"I'm surprised she isn't here already, playing the grande dame and according Lisa a graceful welcome," Luke glanced around in a puzzled way.

"There is an explanation for that."

"Then explain away," frowned Luke. "I hope there have been no family arguments."

"Not what you would call an argument, exactly. More of a compromise. It's like this," she hurried on. "Since Giselle and Jean Claude couldn't come to the wedding, and since Giselle, as you very well know, loves to make a big thing of family occasions, she had arranged a reception for tonight, inviting those of your friends and neighbours who were not able to travel to Scotland."

At Luke's indignant exclamation she went on quickly.

"Giselle wouldn't believe me when I said you might not be in a mood for such a big affair on your first day home. I couldn't talk her out of it. You know as well as I do that once she gets an idea into her head, nothing will stop her, especially," Marguerite's lips sneered, "when it gives her the opportunity to play the part of the chatelaine again."

"Damn," Luke was far from pleased. "I guessed there might be a small family party, but certainly not a large, formal affair."

He was about to lead me to the stairway when Marguerite put out a detaining hand.

"Actually, there is going to be a small family party as well! You see, Giselle told Jamie he was too young to attend the reception tonight, and he was furious. I am sure if he had appreciated that he was the Lord of the Manor, so to speak, he would have put his foot down and insisted on being there. Fortunately he didn't. Giselle is very prickly about her position here and we didn't want her sulking for your home-coming. On the other hand we didn't want Jamie to be miserable either, so Nana came up with the bright idea he should have his own little welcoming party the moment you arrived.

"That smoothed things over, except," she grinned in a way which showed her resemblance to her brother, "being a de la Haie, Jamie insisted that if he couldn't attend Giselle's party, it was only right she shouldn't expect to come to his, so it will only be Nana you will meet this afternoon, Lisa. I've an idea," she twinkled, "that you will be glad of the respite."

From the moment of his excited welcome in the playroom where afternoon tea had been set out, Jamie's party was a huge success. He amused us with his non-stop chatter, he flattered me by showing me his most prized possessions, and he made Luke almost choke when he informed Nana that his uncle had married me because he, Jamie, had wanted me to be his real aunt.

Nana chuckled and smiled at me and replied that she was sure Luke would always go out of his way to make him happy, but she rather doubted that was the main reason why his uncle had chosen me for his wife.

I took to Nana with her placid temperament and cheerful manner. I liked the way she handled Jamie, firmly yet lovingly and I could tell that she reciprocated my feelings from the way she watched me and saw that I was as fond of the little boy as he was of me.

I wasn't so certain that I would enjoy the reception later in the evening. I prefer a small party to a large reception, informality to formality. Moreover, not as yet having met Giselle and her son, Marguerite and Luke would be the only people I would know, and worse still, I would be the centre of interest for a lot of curious eyes.

As I promised Jamie I would come and say goodnight to him later, and followed Luke from the happy atmosphere of the playroom, I wished I could opt out of tonight's affair by pleading a migraine, but he would have guessed I was only making an excuse, taking the coward's way out because I was shy about meeting the other members of the family and their friends, and I didn't want to be thought of as cowardly.

5

I COULDN'T decide what to wear for Giselle's party. I thought the dress Luke suggested might be too formal for the occasion, and I did not want to appear over-dressed. I was dithering and near to tears when there was a knock on the door and Marguerite came into the bedroom.

"Luke says you are as bad as I am at deciding what dress to wear for a party. He sent me to see if I could help. Men," she shook her head, "they don't understand how we feel about clothes."

She rifled through the wardrobe and pulled out a dress.

"This is the one," she decided, holding it out to me. "The colour is perfect. It changes with the light, as your eyes do, from blue to green to grey. It's very stylish and taffeta is the 'in' material this season." She cocked her head at me and inquired. "Was it a honeymoon buy?"

I blushed and nodded. "Luke chose it for me. He wanted me to wear it tonight, but I was afraid it might be a bit too formal."

"This is your night, Lisa. You are expected to steal the limelight, and you definitely will," she went on with generous praise as she helped me slip the gown over my shoulders.

She fastened the minute hooks at the back for me, since my own fingers were too shaky to do so, and then, casting a critical glance at my casual hair-style, she decided to re-arrange it, skilfully swirling my hair into a pile on top of my head to give me added height and at the same time to show off my long slim neck. Then she teased a few curling strands from the top-knot to slightly soften the style, stood back, and nodded approvingly at the final effect.

I was about to stand up, but she

wasn't finished yet. She touched up my make-up, adding a deeper shade of blue gloss to my eye-lids, and when she had finished, she told me to look in the mirror.

I hardly recognised the young woman who stared back at me.

"Well?" she asked.

"Wonderful!" I exclaimed with delight. "Thanks, Marguerite. You've been such a help."

"Just a part payment for what you have done for me," she retorted lightly. "You do know, don't you, that if Luke hadn't met you and persuaded you to marry him, Edouard and I would still be arguing about when, or perhaps if, our own marriage would take place. We have now decided on a June wedding, and I am so happy, Lisa." She dropped an unexpected kiss on my cheek.

"Now," she linked her arm in mine, "Let's go and join Luke before he wears a hole in the living room carpet, pacing up and down waiting for us with his usual impatience."

If I had needed a further boost to my confidence I was given it by the look of admiration in my husband's eyes when Marguerite nudged me ahead of her into the room where he was waiting for us.

"Very nice," he smiled. "Very nice indeed. And you are even on time," he added in mock surprise.

As we followed Marguerite down the great staircase she whispered, "By the way, Lisa, I should have warned you of this earlier, Giselle speaks no English. For the remainder of the evening I'm afraid you will have to converse in French. I hope you will not find it too much of a strain."

Giselle de la Haie was much as I had pictured her to be from Marguerite's description. Tall, slim and dark-haired, with a flawless ivory complexion shown to advantage by the black velvet dress she was wearing, she looked every inch the châtelaine as she came forward to meet me.

Luke introduced us and she held my

hand with her beautifully manicured fingers as she told me how pleased she was to meet me at last.

Her damson black eyes studied me with interest and seemed to like what they saw, before she introduced me to her son Jean Claude, an extremely handsome young man with curly black hair, a superb tan and a practised smile which showed very even, very white teeth as he took my hand in his.

"Enchanté de faire votre connaissance, Lisa," he murmured, making the French equivalent more meaningful by his warm tone and flattering glance.

He seemed reluctant to let go of my hand, but had to do so when Luke very deliberately extended his to say his words of greeting, and then equally deliberately manoeuvred him towards Marguerite, who was looking amused at the by play.

"We are fortunate that Luke and Lisa managed to get here to-day," she engaged him in conversation. "Do you know that because of the blizzard, the airport was closed down. Yours was one of the last planes to land, so I heard on the radio."

"It would have been dreadful if you hadn't got here for this evening!" Giselle looked quite shocked. "It would have been difficult to contact everyone to postpone my little reception for you."

"Your guests might not be able to come themselves, maman," said Jean Claude, mischievously. "It's still snowing, you know."

"Nonsense," she frowned. "They would have telephoned by now if they didn't intend to come."

She turned to me, "My son likes to tease. You mustn't take all that he says to heart," she cast him a reproving look. "Now, while the cousins talk, you come over here with me," she led the way to a silk upholstered divan drawn up in front of the fragrant smelling pine wood fire. "I have been so curious about you," she admitted frankly. "We were all quite taken aback

134

when we were told that Luke was going to marry a girl he had only known for a few days. It was the last thing we expected of him."

"My family felt much the same about me," I admitted. "It worried them, right up to the last minute, until they met Luke."

"It was very romantic, the way you met," Giselle smiled. "Still, one does expect to find romance in Paris, n'est-ce pas? It is a city for lovers," she sighed. "There are times when I still miss living there. I am a Parisienne by birth. I am also a romantic. We have much in common, you and I, Lisa," she spoke quickly, lightly, smiling at me all the time, trying to make me feel at ease, and succeeding, for she was much friendlier than I had expected her to be from the way Luke and his sister had talked of her.

"Yes," her voice chirped on, reminding me of the sparrows of her native city, "my marriage was an equally unexpected love match. I too was swept off my feet within a few days by a handsome de la Haie and brought here to St. Cécile to make my home away from my own family. I too," she spoke more slowly, "had to take on the responsibility of looking after a younger member of the family right from the start, although with me it was rather different. You knew Luke was Jamie's guardian. You knew what you had to take on, but when I married Henri I did not know I was about to become step-mother to a young man only a few years my junior. It was naughty of Henri not to tell me of Alain, but in any case I grew to love him like my own son, just as I have come to love Jamie as a grandson. In fact, I was most surprised, knowing how fond I was of the boy, that Alain didn't make me his guardian. Luke and Marguerite after all are only his second cousins, not really his uncle and aunt as he persists in calling them. Jean Claude is his only true uncle."

"But he likes them better than he

likes you," I almost blurted out the words, and for the first time since Giselle had drawn me aside for this tête-à-tête, I found myself weighing her words.

Why should Jamie dislike her as he did if she was as fond of him as she made out? Was she over-fond, embarrassing him with her affection, or what seemed more likely, was she over strict with him. After all, tonight she could have made an exception to his routine and allowed him to join the party for the hour before dinner. It would have been a special treat for him and he would have enjoyed it.

"Poor little boy," she shook her head, "I feel so sorry for him, losing both his parents in that shocking accident. He can never be a first class skier like the other members of the family." She sighed. "He will be the only de la Haie not to have his name engraved on the St. Cécile trophy."

She got no further for at that moment the manservant Maurice came into the room to announce that the cars bringing the first of the guests were coming up the drive.

With a lithe, graceful movement, Giselle rose to her feet.

"Thank goodness. I was beginning to wonder if Jean Claude was right, and the snow fall had deterred people from leaving home.

"Lisa," she motioned me to get to my feet, "and you too, Luke," she glanced across at my husband, "must stand with me to receive our guests. Come," her voice rang out imperiously. This was the grande dame giving her orders. I tried to hide a smile as I compared her present role with that of the friendly woman who had been telling me of her own love story and of her warm feelings for 'poor little Jamie' only seconds earlier.

Behind her back Luke gave me a wink which as good as said, "How's that for an act?" and any nervousness I might have had disappeared. If Giselle could play her part so stylishly, why

138

shouldn't I? After all, she had cast me in the star role this evening, so why not take up the challenge? Smiling serenely I slipped my arm into Luke's and followed her into the hall.

The guests appeared to be friends of Giselle's rather than the Fletchers. They were middle-aged, apart from the doctor's daughter Arlette, who couldn't keep her infatuated eyes off Jean Claude, and Pierre Duval and his wife Eloise, who were greeted with pleasure by Luke. I recognised Duval's face, having seen it often on television and the sports pages of national newspapers, where his ski-ing abilities made headline news.

"Most of the guests are the local dignitaries," Luke whispered to me when we managed to get a moment together after all the introductions had been made. "They are the kind of people Giselle considers of importance, but they are rather a stuffy lot, apart from Dr. de Vigny and, of course, Pierre and his wife. You will like them. They are both very old friends of mine. Let's join them," he steered me to where they were standing talking to Marguerite while Giselle held court at the far end of the room with the older people.

Eloise Duval studied me with frank curiosity. "We have all been wondering what you would be like," she told me. "You can't be surprised at that, you know. You set all the tongues here wagging for weeks with your romance. Luke had been so clever at evading the marriage trap, we thought he would never be caught," she cast an amused glance at my husband.

"Now that you have met Lisa," Jean Claude, with the doctor's daughter in tow came to join us, "you will understand why. I wish I had met her first," his brown eyes flirted with me.

"He would have said that, no matter whom I had married," Luke stepped between me and his young cousin. "Let me warn you, Lisa, Jean Claude is the family flirt, and a fast worker, so watch out for him.

"Talking of speed," he turned to the other man, "how did you get on in the championship which kept you from attending our wedding?"

"The times were very fast and the course record was broken, but I managed to come in third," Jean Claude looked pleased with himself.

Duval nodded. "You did well. If you keep on improving as you have done this season, I wouldn't be surprised if you are the next member of the family to be invited to represent France in the Winter Olympics."

"He may not be able to do so," said Giselle who had come over to be with us. "When we leave here to make our home in Cannes, it won't be easy for him to put in as much practice on the slopes as he can at present."

"Nonsense," said Luke sharply. "Cannes is at most only a two hour drive away. In any case, Jean Claude will be welcome to come and stay with us any time he wishes."

"That won't be the same," she persisted. "He is going to miss living here as I am going to. He was born here in the Château des Neiges. He has been here all his life."

"Jean Claude will have the time of his life in Cannes," Pierre contradicted her. "Especially when the film festival takes place, and there will be all those lovely girls around. I almost envy him."

"Talking of pretty girls reminds me I've been overlooking my duty," Jean Claude touched Duval's arm. "It's high time we toasted Luke's bride and officially welcomed her to the family, so come along Pierre, help me open the champagne and fill up the glasses."

They had handed the glasses to the guests, who were now standing facing where I stood with Luke, who had put his arm lightly round my waist, when the door opened and a flustered Maurice announced the arrival of another guest.

Eyes switched fr[...] doorway. Luke's finge[...] my waist. Marguerite, b[...] in an audible breath an[...] looked taken aback as tl[...] advanced into the lounge a[...] [...]ng Giselle went forward to me [...]er.

"Forgive me for being so late," the woman kissed Giselle's cheeks. "You can blame the snow. The road over the col was very treacherous, and it is snowing again," she gave a shiver. "I'm lucky to have got here in one piece. You know how I hate driving in this kind of weather."

Her hostess slipped an arm into hers and led her to where I was standing.

"You have already met Frédérique, Lisa," she said. "She was one of the lucky ones who was able to go from here to your wedding in Edinburgh."

"Mais non, Giselle," the woman in the low cut black jersey silk dress contradicted her. "I have not yet met Luke's wife. I had to combine business with pleasure when I was in Scotland, gh I was able to attend the ceremony, alas, I had to miss reception where I would have met the bride."

"Then let me introduce you now. Lisa, this is Frédérique Legrand. I am sure you will have heard Luke and Marguerite mention her. She is a very dear friend of the family as well as being Marguerite's business partner. Frédérique, this is Luke's wife, Lisa."

The woman held out her hand. My acting at this moment would have won me an Oscar, for I held out my hand without a tremor, and my smile remained on my lips although inside I felt cold as ice, and the hairs at the nape of my neck rose with the discomfort I was feeling, for Frédérique Legrand was the woman I had imagined to look at me so malevolently in church on my wedding day, and now I knew that malevolence had been real, for even now, though her lips were parted in what to others must seem a friendly smile, her eyes betrayed her true feelings. For a reason I didn't understand at that moment, this woman disliked me, and where I was concerned, she didn't care if I was aware of the fact.

Seconds later, when she moved past me to greet Luke, with a lingering kiss on his cheeks, I found the reason. She was in love with my husband. She might even have hoped he might marry her one day, but I had come along and put paid to those hopes.

With an effort I kept my smile in position.

"You've arrived just at the right time, Frédérique," Jean Claude's cheerful voice announced. "Here you are," he handed her a glass of champagne, then picked up another one from the tray he had placed on a side table.

Raising it towards me he smiled and said, "To Lisa, may she have health and happiness always."

"To Lisa," the other guests repeated and drank the toast, but although Frédérique raised her glass to her lips,

145

she didn't take a sip.

My fingers tightened round the stem of the glass I had been given but I relaxed them. I mustn't let this woman rile me. More importantly, I mustn't let her see she was riling me. When she deliberately took hold of Luke's arm to murmur something to him which made him smile, I even managed to say lightly.

"I think we should also drink a toast to Luke. I want him to have health and happiness with me!"

The guests laughed approvingly and I raised my glass to Luke, and slowly drank the wine, and let the bubbles which invaded my mouth remind me of our wedding day, our wedding night, and remembering these, my tension ebbed away. This woman, no woman, could spoil my happiness with Luke. I mustn't be jealous or over-possessive, qualities which I didn't admire in others.

All the same, it wasn't easy to keep on smiling while Frédérique continued to hold my husband's arm and keep his attention diverted from me saying.

"I am so glad you didn't take a long holiday just now. If you had, you wouldn't have time to get much training done for the St. Cécile race. You have entered for it, haven't you?"

Without waiting for his reply she glanced at me.

"Are you as keen on ski-ing as Luke?" she wanted to know. "I hope so, for your sake," she smiled blandly. "He likes to spend most of his free times on the high slopes. It's this dedication to the sport which has kept him a champion for so long."

Pierre Duval asked me if I ski-ed.

"We don't get the same opportunities in Scotland as you do here," I shrugged. In the company of a world champion like Pierre I didn't want to boast that I had been the woman's champion of the University Ski Club, knowing that there is a world of difference between even the best British skiers and their French counterparts.

Frédérique's next words took me by surprise. "If you like, I shall teach you," she offered, having erroneously deduced from my reply that I did not ski at all. "You will feel very out of things here if you don't ski."

"That's kind of you, Frédérique," Luke answered for me, "but I think I should be the one to teach Lisa. That is if you would like to learn?" he cocked his head inquiringly.

"I would like to ski well," I agreed.

"In that case, we shall go to the centre tomorrow and get you all the equipment you will need."

Before I could explain Giselle was leading the way across the hall to the dining room.

A flicker of movement near the top of the shadowy staircase caught my attention. I looked up and saw Jamie's face peering through the carved bannister. The sound of the gong had possibly wakened him, and his curiosity had brought him from his room to peek at the visitors.

I nudged Luke, who glanced where I was indicating and smiled at his nephew. The little boy waved back, and apparently satisfied he had seen all he wanted to see, he retreated back to the top of the stairs.

We entered the dining room, a long, panelled room brilliantly lit by two crystal chandeliers whose lights reflected on the white damask cloth, the silver cutlery and the crystal glasses set out below.

Giselle had stopped at the head of the table and was indicating where the guests should sit when a scream of terror made every one jump.

"That's Jamie!" exclaimed Luke, and made to leave the room to find out what was happening, but Giselle put out her hand and stopped him.

"Don't pay any attention," she said sharply. "Jamie is either having one of his nightmares again, in which case Nana knows how to deal with him, although I think it is more likely he is trying to annoy me. He was angry when I told him he was too young to sit up and dine with us tonight, and this is probably his way of getting back at me. You know what he can be like, Luke."

"No, I don't. I haven't had any trouble with him," he brushed aside her detaining hand and had almost reached the door when Jamie himself pushed it open and came in as quickly as his halting gait would let him.

"Luke," he clutched his uncle's arm, "when I went back into my room just now, there was a man there. He was leaning over the bed with something bulky in his hands. I was scared and I couldn't help screaming."

"Of course you couldn't," Luke put a hand on his shoulder.

"Don't be silly, Jamie. How could there be a man in your room? You've been dreaming," snapped Giselle.

"No I wasn't," he glared at her. "There was a man, a big man, but when he heard me scream he got a fright and jumped out of the window."

"Really," Giselle could hardly contain her annoyance. "Now I know you are making up the story."

"I'm not, I'm not. I was frightened and Nana came when I screamed, but I didn't want her, I wanted — " his voice broke and he hurled himself, sobbing, against Luke.

He wanted his mother, I thought, just as he wanted her that day in the park, and now he's remembered she is dead. I felt like crying too, but Giselle was quite unsympathetic.

"Be sensible, Jamie, you know it was only a bad dream you had. Off you go to bed. Nana will be waiting for you."

"No," said Luke firmly. "You stay here for the moment, Jamie. Lisa will look after you," he pushed the little boy gently into my arms. "Pierre and I will go up and investigate."

They returned ten minutes later with Nana.

"Come along, young man," she said in English. "Time you were back in bed. There is no one upstairs now," she assured him, "but just in case you have another bad dream, I've made up the special bed in my room for you."

"Was it really just a dream?" he looked bewildered. "It seemed so real."

"There, there, laddie," she took his hand, "when you're tired and excited it's sometimes difficult to know if you're asleep or awake."

"You were right, Giselle," Frédérique who understood English, remarked. "Nana said he had a nightmare."

"He didn't," said Luke quietly. "There was someone in his room. We found the window wide open and when we looked out we could see tracks in the deep snow below where the intruder had landed when he ran off.

"Should we call the police?" said Dr. De Vigny.

"Not necessary. And I don't want Jamie involved with an investigation again."

6

I ADMIRED the skill with which Giselle firmly steered the conversation from the intruder, saying that this was no topic for a welcome to a new bride.

She turned to me. "My dear, you mustn't let this unusual incident make you chary about living in St. Cécile. You will soon find that it is a delightful place to make your home, although at first you are bound to find our ways a little different from yours, and our food too, perhaps?"

By the time coffee was served in the salon, I felt exhausted and longed to get to bed. It had been a tiring day, with our early morning start, the bumpy and uncomfortable flight, meeting so many strangers, especially Frédérique. Most tiring of all, however, in spite of my fluency, was having to speak in French for the entire evening.

I could feel myself drooping. I muttered a prayer that the guests would soon take their leave. If Luke had been by my side to give me an encouraging smile or an understanding touch of the hand I might have felt less sorry for myself but somehow we hadn't managed to get together after dinner, for the guests were eager to talk to me and ask questions about my homeland which had given Frédérique an opportuniry to continue her lively conversation with my husband, without deliberately appearing to be keeping him from my side.

It was Dr. de Vigny who made the first move to go. He saw me turn aside to stifle a yawn, and possibly his professional eyes had noticed my growing weariness, for he gave me a sympathetic smile, and beckoned his daughter, who was still clinging to Jean Claude, to come over to join him.

"It's time we were going, my dear," he told her. "If we delay much longer, we may not get back to St. Cécile. When Maurice brought in fresh logs just now, he told me that it has started to snow again quite heavily."

"You are very wise, Dr. de Vigny," the local mayor, whose name kept slipping from my mind, agreed with him. "I think we should all be on our way. We don't want to become stranded in a snow drift, do we?"

Only Frédérique made no move, but continued to talk to Luke and Jean Claude. She lingered on long after all her fellow guests had left, until Marguerite suggested she shouldn't delay her departure in case the snow grew heavier.

"I'm such a coward," she smilingly confessed to Giselle. "I've been putting off leaving, because I don't relish the idea of driving on my own over the pass on a night like this."

"Why not stay the night here, as you often do?" suggested Giselle. "I am sure Marguerite won't mind preparing a bedroom for you in her wing."

"No. That's out of the question tonight. I have to be in Geneva for lunch tomorrow with a possible new client. It would be an important commission, as Marguerite knows, and I don't want to be late for the appointment. I must get home to get the necessary papers, and to change, of course," she laughed. "I could hardly attend a business lunch dressed like this."

"I don't know about that," joked Luke. "If your business is with a man, I'm sure he would approve."

"I would offer to drive you home," Jean Claude didn't sound over enthusiastic, "but I don't think maman would trust me with her Mercedes on a night like this."

"And I wouldn't trust myself to your driving," retorted Frédérique. She turned to me with a pleading smile. "As a matter of fact, Lisa, Luke usually drives me home when the weather is bad. I am sure you wouldn't mind him doing so again tonight, would you? He would be back in an hour."

"Don't be silly," Marguerite spoke quickly. "Luke is still on his honeymoon. If I was his wife I would be most offended if he walked off with another woman even if she was an old friend of the family.

"You needn't worry, though. I shall drive you back to Vallon. In any case, I'm a better driver than he is, so you will be safer with me," she grinned at her brother. "By the time you have had another coffee, I shall have changed and packed an overnight bag, since I might as well stay with you rather than make the return trip on my own."

I could have hugged her. I knew she hadn't been over pleased about her brother's whirlwind romance, but she had accepted his decision to marry, had been more than delighted when she had realised that it had made it possible for her to marry her Edouard without further arguments, and now perhaps felt she owed me some kind of thanks for being instrumental in bringing about her return to happiness.

I snuggled contentedly in Luke's arms that night. He kissed my eyelids closed.

Breakfast was what I guessed it would be. Coffee, hot croissants, and lots of butter and cherry jam. I lingered lazily over it, while Luke attended to mail which had arrived during his absence.

He frowned over one letter.

"Is there something wrong?"

"I'll have to go to Cannes for a couple of days next week."

"I've never been to Cannes."

"This is a business trip. I'll be tied up all the time. You might as well stay here and get to know your way around."

"I thought your business was connected with that paper mill we passed."

"Not for much longer. I thought I had mentioned that Marguerite and I have sold our interest in it?"

"Darling, I've had so much on my mind, so many things to try and take

158

in that I haven't followed everything you've told me. I know you have something to do with a paper mill. I know you look after Jamie's estate for him, and you did mention something about alterations to the Château. I know you have a house you inherited from your mother, and father did seem satisfied that you would be able to keep me in the luxury to which you," I smiled at him, "are accustomed, but truth to tell, I'm not very sure what you actually do."

"My mother inherited the de la Haie paper mill in St. Cécile from her father, and when she died Marguerite and I became the joint owners, but neither of us were interested in the business. However, on my uncle's advice, I learned about it, and after taking a course in management, I took over the working of it. It's a very prosperous business and I made it even more prosperous but my heart was never in it.

"My uncle also had another venture

in mind, although Giselle opposed this. He was finding the Château too large and too expensive to maintain as it should be maintained. Alain suggested to him that it should be converted into a luxury hotel, with the family maintaining one of the wings as their private residence. St. Cécile is a popular centre for both winter sports and summer visitors who come to see the wild flowers for which the valley is famous, to fish in the lakes and rivers, to climb, to enjoy the amenities of the sports centre with its swimming pool and tennis courts. A château-hotel with the Count as host would have a certain snob appeal," he grimaced.

"Uncle died before the venture was off the drawing board, but Alain set the wheels in motion. The plans had been approved the month before the accident, and it was then that Marguerite and I decided to sell the paper mill and invest some of our money in Alain's scheme, which we both thought of as something we would like to be involved in. The idea was that Alain would retain one wing of the place as his own private dwelling. The rest would be made over to the company we would form. The three directors, Alain, Marguerite and myself would have equal shares in it, and I was to be managing director.

"Nothing had been finalised when Alain had his accident, but when he was in hospital he signed the necessary papers for the go ahead. He didn't want Jamie to inherit a pile of bricks and mortar which would only be a burden to him. He wanted him to have a worthwhile inheritance, his own home, and a share in a hotel which would be a money spinner and in which he hoped Jamie would take an active interest when he was older."

"What about Giselle? Does she have a say?"

"No. She has no claims on the Château and nor does Jean Claude. Alain as the first born inherited the castle and the estates around it, including the pine forests, which are now Jamie's. Giselle inherited Uncle Henri's villa in Cannes and an adequate sum of money. Jean Claude inherited the smaller de la Haie estate, a small house with a large and well managed vineyard in the hills behind Cannes. Neither had anything to complain about, although Giselle isn't too pleased at having to leave the Château, which under the terms of that will she had to do if she hadn't already done so, by Jean Claude's eighteenth birthday in June."

There was a knock on the door. It was Nana to tell us that the police had arrived.

Both officers were very pleasant. Jamie was questioned so tactfully he was made to think that what had happened was an exciting adventure rather than something frightening, a story to put him one up on his young friends in the village. They explained to him about taking fingerprints, and took his own, much to his delight.

As Luke and Pierre had assumed the previous evening, both officers were of the opinion that the man, having heard either at the ski centre or in the village inn that there was a party at the Château, had taken advantage of the fact and had slipped into the house when the door was opened for the guests, in the hope that there might be some easy pickings in the bedrooms where he thought he would be unlikely to be disturbed while the dinner party was in progress. He couldn't have been a local man, or he would have known there was a youngster in the house who wouldn't be downstairs with the adults, and he would have got as big a fright as Jamie when the boy surprised him in the bedroom.

It was a lovely week. There was no more snow, only brilliant sunshine. The roads around St. Cécile had been swept clear, leaving hillocks of snow on either side, and Luke was able to drive me to places of interest in the vicinity, as well as to St. Cécile itself where he pointed out the shops I would frequent, and Dr. de Vigny's house, and the local church, which dated back to the middle ages, and had a famous triptych.

One day when we were driving past the Villa des Narcisses, I glanced towards it wistfully and asked Luke how soon we would be able to move in.

"I had hoped the present tenants would move out before their lease expired at the end of February. When I told them I would not be renewing it, they said they would leave the moment they found something suitable in the neighbourhood but so far nothing has turned up, so now I don't expect they will leave until their lease expires."

He shot me a swift glance. "Aren't you happy at the Château?"

"Of course I am. Although Marguerite goes out of her way to make me feel at home, however, I am always conscious that it is her home as much as yours. In any case, Luke, I have been longing to see over the Villa since the first day you pointed it out to me."

"Even if it was vacant, Lisa, we wouldn't be moving in right away. It is in need of redecoration."

"I know. Marguerite told me. That's something I'm looking forward to, deciding what I want done, deciding on colour schemes. Redecorating our home will give me plenty to do when you are at work all day."

"You needn't worry about the re-decoration, Lisa. Frédérique is going to see to it. Didn't Marguerite tell you so?"

I looked at him, frowning. "There is some misunderstanding. Marguerite knows I intend to do it myself. We have even discussed one or two ideas together, and she has given me a list of places where I gan get what materials and fabrics I want."

"Don't you think you should leave such a big job to an expert?" Luke seemed dubious of my ability. "It was kind of Frédérique to offer when she has other contracts on hand, but it is a project she is very interested in."

"I am sure she is," I replied drily, "but so am I. I shall enjoy working on it, and after all, Les Narcisses is to be my home, isn't it? If I am to live there, I want it to be as I want it, a reflection of my personality, not someone else's."

Luke shook his head. "Frédérique is going to be disappointed, but if that's how you feel about it, there is no more to be said. If you do need help, however, I'm sure she will be willing to give it."

"If she is good at painting ceilings, she could give me a hand there. It's my unfavourite decorating job."

"I don't think I'll suggest that to her," his lips quirked. "Manual work isn't exactly her line, and it is not going to be yours either," he said firmly.

I hadn't expected Frédérique to be pleased when Luke told her he wasn't going to commission her to do the job at the villa, but I was completely taken aback by the fury of her reaction.

It wasn't Luke she flared up at

when he told her of our decision when she dropped in the following Sunday, ostensibly to discuss some project with Marguerite. That day she merely shrugged and said if that's how we wanted it, so be it. She waited until Monday, when she knew Luke would be back at the mill where he had outstanding business to attend to before the new firm took over, and when she knew Marguerite had gone to Grenoble to see a client, before she revealed her true feelings.

Maurice announced her arrival to me at mid-morning, when I was having elevenses with Jamie and Nana in the playroom.

"I've shown Mademoiselle Legrand into your living room," he told me. "Would you like me to serve coffee there?"

"Thank you, Maurice, that is kind of you. I am sure my visitor will appreciate a cup."

"You won't be with her all morning, will you?" pouted Jamie. "You promised you would take me to St. Cécile before lunch so that I could help you choose some postcards for your friends in Scotland."

"I shouldn't be long, Jamie," I smiled, but my heart was fluttering nervously. I had a good idea that this was not a social call and I wondered what the other woman wanted to say to me.

She didn't leave me long in doubt. She didn't even wait for Maurice to set the tray down on the coffee table before she began her angry harangue. As usual she treated him as if he didn't exist, much as she treated Nana and anyone else she considered in an inferior position.

"You may think you are a very clever young woman, Lisa, but I am not going to let you get away with what you have done."

Maurice discreetly left the room, but without closing the door, as she stormed on.

"You knew from Marguerite, didn't

you, that Luke was going to marry me, until you came along and pretended such a kindly, motherly interest in Jamie, although I expect you really dislike the little brat as much as I do.

"Yes. You saw Luke as a good catch, didn't you? He was rich, good-looking, someone who would give you the kind of life you had only dreamed of until you met him. He was a man who was rather at a loss how to entertain a small boy on holiday in Paris, and after your accidental meeting, you played on that, and on his love for Jamie, to make him notice you.

"If I had known what was going on, I wouldn't have played my hand the way I did, but I never thought he would be faithless to me. Luke and I, you understand, had known each other for years and had been more than friends," she eyed me to see what the impact of her insinuation would be, but I was too taken aback by her tirade to do more than stare at her gape mouthed.

"Everyone, yes, everyone, took it for

granted that once Luke decided to settle down, he would regularise the situation," she glared at me.

I continued to look at her as if she had taken leave of her senses. No sane woman would speak to a new bride as she was speaking to me. Her tone, her manner, her words, were outrageous, and at last finding my tongue, I snapped at her.

"If what you say is true, why didn't Luke ever ask you to marry him? I am sure you wouldn't have refused. But he didn't ask you, did he? He didn't want you for his wife."

"He did, he did," she shrilled, "but he was waiting for Marguerite to get married first. He knew I did not want the responsibility of Jamie, and because he loved me he wouldn't saddle me with the child. We had hoped to settle things when we were all in Paris in October, but I was called home unexpectedly and that very day Marguerite had a hysterical turn. She said she would throw herself in the river if Edouard wouldn't marry her. Knowing Marguerite as I do, I knew it was all play acting, but poor Luke believed her, and he was so worried in case she carried out her threat, that when he met you that afternoon he proposed to you, thinking this was the only way he could help his sister.

"He knew," she sneered, "you wouldn't turn him down. His was too good an offer to refuse."

I gasped with indignation and was about to speak but she did not give me the opportunity.

"Marguerite was very upset. She felt she had driven him to taking his foolish step and right up until the very week of the wedding we all tried to stop him making a fool of himself. I even told him I no longer minded taking on the responsibility of looking after Jamie, but he ignored our every plea.

"We then wondered if you had some hold over him," her eyes swept insultingly over me. "I certainly wondered if all that virginal white at the wedding was as much of a farce as the wedding itself."

Her shrill voice was so loud I was afraid it would carry through the open door and along the corridor to the playroom and this added to my anger.

"Get out," I flared at her. "Get out of this house. You will never be welcome here again when I tell Luke all you have said to-day and how you have insulted me."

She backed away from me, but she still hadn't finished speaking.

"I would deny everything you said, and he would believe me, not you. I would say you had made everything up, out of spite, because you were jealous of me; because you had found out he loved me, and he still does, Lisa. Haven't you noticed the way his eyes follow me? Haven't you noticed when I am in a room, he always comes over to me? He is still in love with me, Lisa, and he is my man. I am not going to give him up. Soon, very soon, he will get tired of being tied to a po-faced little gold-digger like you.

"I'll get him back, Lisa. One way or another, I'll get him back."

With that, she turned quickly on her heel and left the room. I could hear the tattoo of her stiletto heels on the wooden staircase, and long after she had slammed the front door behind her I stood in the middle of the living room shocked and distressed by the scene, certain there had been no truth in some of the things she had said, yet knowing I could never repeat her tirade to Luke or anyone to get her vile words out of my thoughts. They were the outpourings of a woman crazed with jealousy and I shouldn't take them seriously, yet her final words, spoken with such venom, still echoed in my ears, and sent a tingle of apprehension down my spine.

7

I WAS taut with anger when I returned to the playroom, worrying now not so much for myself as for Jamie. Frédérique's high pitched voice would have been audible as far along the corridor as this when all the doors were open, as they had been, and I could guess what the little boy's feelings would be if he had overheard what the angry woman had said about him.

Fortunately only Nana was in the big, airy room where I had been enjoying elevenses when Frédérique had asked to see me. Even if she had overheard the tirade, she would not have understood a word the French girl had said, although she would have guessed from her tone that the conversation had been far from amiable.

Nana turned round as I entered the room, and frowned.

"You look upset, Lisa. What has that young woman been saying to you?" Her tone indicated that she wasn't overfond of Frédérique.

"She is annoyed because I wouldn't give her the contract to redecorate Les Narcisses."

"Why should she be? It is to be your home, not hers. Surely she can appreciate your taste could be quite different from hers, but of course," she sighed, "Frédérique has always liked getting her own way and if she sets her heart on a thing, she must have it. She is not a girl who likes to come off second best. That's why she never competes in ski-ing events with Marguerite," she added with a touch of malice. "She would be a poor loser."

A poor loser. I controlled a shiver. How clearly I had been shown that to-day by Frédérique herself. But I mustn't let her upset me. That would be playing into her hands. I must put the bitter scene from my mind.

175

I must forget all those wild threats, the disturbing innuendoes.

"Where is Jamie?" I forced brightness into my voice. "We still have time to go to St. Cécile this morning, as I promised him."

"I sent him off to wash his hands and get ready to go out with you. Ah, here he is," she looked past me with a smile as the boy, his face rosy with scrubbing, a woollen hat pulled well down over his ears right to the upturned collar of his padded jacket, returned to the playroom.

Because it was a school holiday, because I was taking him out as a special treat, he was in a happy mood, and his chatter as I drove cautiously down the twisty road to the village gave me no time to brood over what Frédérique had screamed at me. However, once the excitement of helping him choose a present for a school friend was over and we sat in the local inn drinking hot chocolate, my thoughts returned to her words.

She had sown a tiny seed of doubt in my mind.

Thinking back, it could have been Frédérique to whom Marguerite had been referring; Frédérique who had wilfully left Luke on his own to cope with Jamie during that holiday to let him see how much she resented having the little boy around; Frédérique who had, on her own admission, hoped he would give in to her and leave guardianship of Jamie to Edouard and Marguerite.

I stared dully into the dark liquid in front of me. Looking back, all of Frédérique's angry outpourings could be true, but were they? Had I allowed my love to over-rule my common sense, grasping eagerly at the chance of marrying the man who had come to mean so much to me? Had I been living in a dream world? Was our marriage only one of convenience as far as Luke was concerned?

He had treated me with affection. He had promised on our wedding day to love me. He had made love to me since then with passion and with tenderness, but never, no, never, had he said those three magical words, 'I love you.'

Why not? Because he was too honest? Because he couldn't say them when he loved another woman?

Damn Frédérique for making me think along those lines. I stirred the hot chocolate with such vigour it slopped over the side of the mug. Damn her for sowing seeds of suspicion in my mind.

I turned to Jamie who was happily munching a wedge of cake, staring out of the window as he did so and muttering between bites the makes of the passing cars, loudly drawing my attention to Giselle's black Mercedes as it swept past the cafe.

"It's time we were on our way home, or you will be late for lunch," I glanced at my watch. "Nana will give me a ticking off if you are."

Nana wasn't in a fit state to worry about our lateness in arriving back at the Château. Marguerite came hurrying out to meet us when we stopped in the cobbled yard, to tell us that Nana wasn't well, and that Jamie shouldn't go and see her in case he too caught 'flu.

"She has a very high temperature, Lisa, and Dr. de Vigny says she should be kept in bed for three or four days."

Nana wasn't the only one to catch the bug. By night-time my sister-in-law also had a high fever, and for the next few days I was kept busy attending to her and Nana, giving them medicines, tidying their beds, carrying trays of light nourishment which I prepared myself, and keeping an eye on Jamie, making sure he wasn't left too often to his own devices. By night time I was exhausted, ready to go to bed the moment dinner had been served.

I saw very little of Luke during these days. He too was busy. Some hitches had cropped up in connection with the sale of the family paper mill. One of the new owners, the senior partner, was a Canadian who was presently in Vancouver trying to negotiate the sale of a mill there, and since Vancouver time differed from Grenoble time by several hours, Luke often had to stay late at the office to take 'phone calls. Often I was asleep before he came home.

The first day that Marguerite was up and about I was giving her afternoon tea in our living room when Luke arrived back unexpectedly. We were given only the curtest of greetings before he hurried across the room to his desk, where he riffled through the papers which were lying there.

"Lisa," he turned to me with an annoyed expression, "where the devil did you put that letter that came this morning. How often must I tell you not to touch my mail."

Niggled by his tone I snapped back. "The letter is where you put it yourself before you dashed out this morning. On the bedside table."

I'd hardly finished speaking before he brushed past me and went striding from the room.

I almost giggled with relief when a couple of minutes later Luke returned to the living room holding the letter and giving me a sheepish grin.

"I'm sorry, Lisa. I shouldn't have spoken to you like that. It's just that I'm on edge with so many things on my mind at the moment, and I couldn't remember what I had done with this letter. I thought I had taken it with me to the office this morning and was worried when I couldn't find it there. Then when I couldn't find it on my desk here, I simply blew up."

"It must be a very important letter."

"It is. It has changed my timetable completely. Instead of going to Cannes next week, as I had intended, I have to be there this evening. I've spent most of today juggling with appointments."

"You're going to Cannes tonight?" I stared at him.

"I must. That letter was from a very good friend of mine who was to be speaker at an important meeting. Unfortunately he has had to go into hospital and I was the one person he thought of as being able to deputise for him. It was unfortunate that the letter was delayed by the postal strike, or I would have had much more notice."

"He should have telephoned."

"He wasn't to know there would be a strike. He wrote because he wanted to give me notes about the subject under discussion. That's why I was upset when I thought I had mislaid the letter."

"You've found it now, so you can calm down," I gave him a quick kiss to show I'd forgiven him. "A cup of tea will help too. There is still some in the pot. After we've had one together, I'll go and do our packing."

"Our packing?" he frowned.

"I'm coming with you, of course."

"No," he shook his head. "Not this time, Lisa. I have far too much business to attend to to have any time to spare for you."

"But — "

"No," he interrupted firmly. "Knowing you were hanging round the hotel on your own would distract me, and I can't afford to be distracted. Don't look so glum, chérie," he added hastily. "I shall have some free time at the end of the month, so I shall take you to Nice for Carnival week. That is something you will enjoy."

"Luke," I pouted, still not pleased at the idea of his going away without me, "you can't be busy all the time. What about in the evenings?"

"Tonight there will be the talk, after that I shall be working late each evening to fit in everything I have to do. No, Lisa. This time you stay at home. You will have to keep an eye on Jamie for me, with Nana still laid up."

"Jamie!" I turned on him, his concern for the boy sharply reminding me of Frédérique's angry assertions. "You make me wonder at times if you married me because you wanted a stand-in mother for the boy and not because you wanted a wife."

With tears starting from my eyes I stormed from the living room, almost colliding with Marguerite who was coming along the corridor. One look at my face stopped her from saying what she had opened her mouth to say to me and I rudely pushed past her to make for the bathroom, the one room in this shared wing of the castle where I could be sure of privacy.

When I came out, some ten minutes later, the tear stains rinsed from my cheeks with cold water, it was to find Luke in the bedroom packing his suitcase. He immediately dropped the items he was holding onto the bed and came forward to take me in his arms.

"Darling, I'm sorry," he kissed my cheeks. "I know you are disappointed at not coming with me, and believe me, I would like to have you with me, but it is quite out of the question. I have too much on my mind, too many appointments to fit into the few days shall be away, that I simply won't have a moment to myself."

"I realise that now, Luke. I was being selfish, not thinking the thing through. It was wrong of me to fly off the handle as I did, but," I sighed, "we have seen so little of one another this past week, with one thing and another, that the thought of five days when I wouldn't even be able to smile at you across the breakfast table, upset me." I stood on tiptoe and kissed his lips lingeringly. "I don't like the idea of being away from you."

"I don't want to be away from you either, chérie," he nibbled my lips, "but believe me, if you came with me this time, when I have so much trouble on my plate, I would be so grumpy with you for any moments we could snatch together, that you might come to wish you had never married me."

"I would never wish that!" I exclaimed fervently.

Later that afternoon I kissed him

goodbye before he got into his car to drive to Cannes.

Marguerite who had come out into the yard with me to wish her brother a safe and successful journey, slipped an arm round my waist.

"Don't look so gloomy, Lisa," she cajoled me. "Luke hasn't gone off to the ends of the earth. He will be back on Saturday, or sooner if he can possibly manage it," she led me back into the castle. "He won't want to miss another week-end's ski-ing if he can possibly help it, and talking of ski-ing," she chattered on, "I have an idea. After lunch tomorrow we shall go shopping at the ski centre. Luke never did get round to taking you there to buy you those ski outfits he promised you, so tomorrow we'll do something about them."

"There's Jamie," I frowned. "He is on holiday tomorrow and I promised I would take him sledging in the afternoon."

"That's no problem," Marguerite had

made up her mind about our outing. "He knows lots of the youngsters who go to the centre. He can go sledging with them while we shop. I'll ask Yves, he is the ski instructor, to keep an eye on him. He is used to doing it for Luke when he takes Jamie to the centre, and Jamie rather hero worships Yves, so you will have no problems."

She was quite right. Jamie made no demur at the change of plans and the following afternoon we left him chatting happily with Yves and a group of youngsters most of whom he knew, while Marguerite and I made for the shopping precinct.

As in the majority of fashionable ski resorts, the sports shops seemed to cater mainly for the well-to-do who liked having an exclusive name tag on their clothes. The prices made me gasp, and although several outfits took my fancy, I told Marguerite that they were all much too expensive and that I would wait until my trunks from home arrived with my own ski-ing gear.

She nodded and said with a smile, "You did rather mislead us the other evening, didn't you? You let us assume that you didn't know much about ski-ing, although just now I guessed from the knowledgeable way you were discussing ski waxes with the assistant that you aren't a complete novice. I am right, am I not?"

"I was a member of the University team, but that was years ago, and I haven't done much ski-ing since. I managed a little in Switzerland when I was working there, but we haven't had a great deal of snow in Scotland these past four winters and I'm very rusty. In any case," I glanced at the towering mountains behind us, "the runs I'm accustomed to are not as long and steep as the ones you use here. My standard will be nothing like as good as yours."

"Don't be so Britishly modest," she shook her head. "I am sure with a little practice you will soon be as good as most of the women I ski with. I tell you what," she decided, "after you have bought those outfits you have been casting admiring glances at, we'll go and have a word with Yves. I am sure he will fit you in for a refresher course this week while Luke is away, so that you can surprise my brother with your skill when he comes home at the week-end."

She signalled imperiously to the shop girl. "Madame Fletcher would like to try on this and this and this," she went from rack to rack selecting the garments she had seen me take an interest in, "and I shall try these ones here myself."

"Marguerite, no!" I gasped. "I can't afford these prices."

"Luke can," she smiled at me. "I have already told you he has an account here. As his wife, you will be expected to keep up appearances, you know."

"But to spend so much on clothes," I shook my head. "I can't."

"You can and you must," she said firmly, then chuckled as she added, a pleased look in her eyes. "Do you know, you have just proved me right yet again.

"What do you mean?"

"One of Luke's disappointed female friends has been hinting to all and sundry that you were a gold digger who married Luke for his money."

"That's nonsense. I had no idea how well off Luke was when he asked me to marry him. I would have married him if he hadn't had a penny to his name. I married him because I love him, just as you love Edouard. Once I had met Luke, I knew there could be no one else for me."

"You don't need to tell me that, chérie. I have watched how you look at him. I have watched Luke, and never have I seen him so relaxed, so at one with anyone. You are right for each other, although, I must confess that I was worried at first. Yours was such a whirlwind romance, quite out of character for Luke.

"As a matter of fact," she went on

slowly, "we had all thought that when he eventually decided to settle down it would be with the daughter of one of our local families, but as usual, Luke didn't conform."

She disappeared into the cubicle next to mine to try on the clothes she had selected for herself, while I digested what she said. Firmly I turned my attention to the clothes the attendant had hung in the cubicle and selected two very lovely outfits. We then returned to the coffee shop which overlooked the nursery slopes on the other side of the main road, where Jamie was sledging.

Marguerite knew several of the women who were gossiping over the coffee cups and one group waved to her to come and join them.

I was rather enjoying myself when there was a sudden lull in the conversation and the group of women turned to stare towards the entrance. I had my back to it and didn't trouble to turn round, assuming that the newcomer was a friend of my new acquaintances and not someone I myself knew. Every nerve in my body tensed when Frédérique's voice close behind me said.

"There you are Marguerite. Nana told me the family had come here for the afternoon. Where has Luke got to?" her eyes swept the café as she drew a chair from another table and insinuated herself between Marguerite and Arlette, whom I would have described as the cattiest of the group. "Did he get tired of watching your efforts on the nursery slopes, Lisa, and go off on his own to the championship run?"

She signalled to a waiter to bring her a coffee and continued without giving me time to reply. "When I have finished my drink, I'll go and join him. You won't mind, will you?" she challenged.

Arlette giggled. "You are going to have to go a long way to catch up on Luke, chérie."

"What do you mean?"

"He isn't here to-day. He has gone off to Cannes for a few days on business."

After a momentary pause Frédérique shot me a swift, sly glance. "Isn't that the oddest thing," she remarked. "I'm going to Cannes on business myself tomorrow."

"Frédérique, you can't!" exclaimed Marguerite. "You know I arranged for you to meet the Rousseaus in Grenoble tomorrow."

"You got my appointments muddled, I'm afraid," shrugged Frédérique. "I had already arranged to look over Giselle's villa when I saw your note in the appointment book about the Rousseaus."

"You should consult me before you make any appointments," Marguerite was angry. "You know the Rousseaus are important clients who bring us a lot of business. You could have postponed Giselle's arrangement. After all, she has waited long enough to make up her mind about when she intends to move into the villa in Cannes. Another day would have made no difference where she is concerned."

"That's not how Luke sees it," Frédérique shot me another oblique glance. "When I was talking to him yesterday he was telling me how worried he was that Giselle still hadn't made any plans for her move to Cannes. To please him I had a word with her and she then asked me to look over the villa, see what needed doing and when that was decided, I was to go ahead with the job. She said I had carte blanche to do the place over from the attic to cellar as I saw fit, and no expense spared."

Again she gave me a sly glance before turning to Marguerite and saying, "I imagine I shall be in Cannes for the rest of the week, seeing to things. I shall be staying at the Reserve if you need to contact me."

"The Reserve?" Arlette raised her eyebrows. "Your expenses come high, don't they?"

Frédérique shrugged. "I always stay

at the Reserve when I visit Cannes. You and Luke do too, don't you Marguerite?"

She was trying to needle me and rather than sit where I was and listen to her, I put down my coffee cup and glanced at my sister-in-law.

"Marguerite, I think it's time we went for Jamie. He will be getting tired and hungry by now, I should imagine."

"You fetch him, Lisa. I should like to have a word with Frédérique about this proposed trip to Cannes," Marguerite was frowning. "Bring him back here for a hot chocolate. That will please him. And by the way, confirm the times of your coaching with Yves. He didn't make a note of them in his appointment book, and knowing Yves, he could forget to fill them in and make another booking."

"What's this about your having coaching with Yves?" Frédérique looked at me angrily. "I understood I was to give you your first ski-ing lesson."

"Lisa isn't a beginner," Marguerite smiled. "She was being over modest about her ski-ing when we discussed it with her. I have only now learned that she skied for her University Club, but because she has had no practice for a couple of years she thinks she wouldn't be up to our standard and I suggested a few lessons with Yves would renew her confidence."

Frédérique eyed me narrowly. It was apparent that she was not at all pleased to learn I was not a ski-ing novice, but she made no comment, except to say, when I had pushed my chair back and was about to leave.

"It really is a shame, Lisa, that Luke has gone off and left you to your own devices so soon. Didn't he want you to go with him to Cannes?"

"Luke has gone to Cannes on business. It wasn't worth my while going with him for all the time we would have had together. Now I must go. Jamie will think we have forgotten him." I turned to Marguerite. "We should be back in ten minutes. I'll pop his sledge in the boot of the car before we return here."

I moved away quickly, but wasn't out of ear-shot when Arlette said in her carrying voice.

"I think your sister-in-law is very trusting to let a man like Luke go off on his own for even a night, Marguerite. If he was my husband, business or no business, I wouldn't have let him leave me behind. Cannes is always full of pretty girls looking for a flirtation, and you know what men are like."

Your kind of man, maybe, I thought, but not mine. Not Luke. No, not Luke, I repeated firmly to myself. Frédérique's arrival at the café, her malicious glances when she had announced that she too was going to Cannes and staying at the Reserve, followed by Arlette's sneering insinuation had combined to detract from what had been until then a most pleasant afternoon.

I tried to recapture my earlier mood

as I watched Jamie cavorting happily with his small friends and listening to his voice raised high with excitement when he won a short race on his sledge. Then I went with Yves to his office to confirm the times of my lessons.

When this was done we went together to where the children were sledging and I called to Jamie it was time to leave. Yves accompanied us to the road, where we stood between an opening in the banks of snow, chatting while we waited for a lull in the traffic to allow us to cross to the car park beside the cafe on the other side.

Jamie still clutching his sledge and Yve's hand, was showing off by reciting the names of the cars which sped past, Mercedes, BMWs, Fiats, Citroens, a Mini which looked like a match box beside the long, low scarlet Ferrari, driven by a girl with long, golden hair, which followed it.

There were no cars behind the Ferrari and Jamie made to step into the road, but Yves held him back.

"Not yet, mon brave. There is a blue Citroen coming up the hill. After that, all is clear."

The Citroen passed. We stepped out from between the piled up snow at the side onto the road. Just at that moment a car drove at speed from the car park opposite. It hit against the bank of snow at the exit, then went into a skid which the driver seemed unable to control. In his panic he must have stepped on the accelerator pedal, for the car suddenly swooped broadside across the road, coming towards us with an impetus which would have knocked us to the ground if Yves, quicker to react than I was, hadn't grabbed at both Jamie and me and dragged us back to the safety of the snow barrier at the roadside. Jamie cried out as he dropped his sledge in the roadway, but Yves ignored him and pushed us both behind the snow mound. Seconds later the car hit it, and its bumper rasped noisily against the frozen wall of white, sending slivers of ice and snow flying in all directions. There was a cracking sound as the wheels went over the little sledge, and then, somehow, the driver brought his vehicle under control, and without waiting to see if anyone had been hurt by his carelessness, he went racing off down the hill and out of sight.

Yves was muttering words which were not included in my French vocabulary, but whose meaning I could guess at. He glanced first at me and then at Jamie, anxiety in his eyes. Jamie was trembling, but it was with rage rather than fear as I realised when he kept shouting.

"My sledge! That silly man ran over my sledge. Look, he has broken it to pieces!"

He tried to pull away from Yves, but the man held him back and looked at me again.

"Are you all right, Madame Fletcher?"

"Yes, thanks to you." My voice shook as I added, quietly, turning from Jamie so that he wouldn't hear my words.

"We could have been killed if you hadn't acted so quickly," I shuddered, my eyes now on the smashed sledge. "People who drive like that in these conditions shouldn't be allowed on the road."

"Tourists," muttered Yves. "There are always accidents when they come here in winter. They have no idea how to drive in snow conditions."

"He could drive well enough when it came to making his get away," I snapped, anger overcoming fright as I looked from the broken sledge to Jamie's tear stained face. "I wish I had been able to stop him and make him pay for his carelessness. Jamie treasured that sledge, but don't cry, Jamie," I slipped an arm round the boy's shoulder, "I shall buy you another one. A wooden one, this time, with proper runners. How about that?"

The snuffling stopped abruptly. Jamie turned and looked up at me, eyes sparkling now with delight as well as tears.

"A wooden sledge? A real wooden sledge?"

I nodded. "If we go back to Yves's sports shop, perhaps he will help us choose one now?" I glanced at the man beside me.

"But of course," he agreed, giving me approving looks, knowing, as I knew, that the excitement of buying a new sledge would erase the scene from his mind.

8

AFTER dinner on the evening of the day Frédérique had gone off to Cannes, Marguerite remarked to Giselle how annoyed she had been at the change of arrangements.

"Frédérique should consult me about any appointments. I didn't even know you were thinking of having your new villa redecorated until she told me of it, and to go off the way she did was most upsetting."

Giselle looked at her in surprise. "You can't be annoyed with me Marguerite. I didn't know she hadn't told you about our arrangement, and in any case, I wasn't expecting her to put off her other engagements to suit me. I told her there was no hurry to see over the villa."

"That's not what she inferred," Marguerite frowned.

When I went to bed that night I tried not to think about Frédérique and her deliberate pursuit of Luke to Cannes, where she would be able to meet him, aware that I would not be able to prevent her from doing so. Yet what could she gain by this manoeuvre? If Luke was so busy that he hadn't had time to spare for me, he wasn't likely to alter his plans to suit Frédérique, yet the thought that they were both under the same roof and that she was determined by hook or crook to win him back, niggled me. I didn't sleep well and by morning my head ached, I felt dispirited and sour tempered and it wasn't until late afternoon, after an exhilirating session on the slopes, that I managed to regain my usual good humour.

To my delight, Luke telephoned me late that night.

"How are things with you, chérie?"

"I do miss you darling, but at least, with your not being here, I've managed to complete the final draft of my travel book. If you approve of it, I'll send it off to my agent. When will you be home to read it?"

"I'm not sure yet. It depends how things go, but I am hoping to be home for the week-end so that I can get in some ski-ing practice. I was on the 'phone to Jean Claude earlier to-day. We had some business to discuss, and he reminded me that our local championship is in a fortnight's time. He even talked of beating me, and I can't have that!"

"So it's for ski-ing you are going to hurry home?"

"What else?" there was amusement in his voice. "After all, ski-ing was my first love."

'And am I your last?' I almost spoke the words aloud —

I spent another restless night, but with the light of day, somehow things didn't seem so bad. I told myself I had been letting my imagination run away with me. Luke was my husband and no way would I let another woman

205

take him from me. I determinedly filled my hours with work, helping Nana with mending, discussing ideas for the new decor of both the Château and Les Narcisses with Marguerite, and ski-ing for hours the first three afternoons of Luke's absence, until I exhausted myself, but I earned Yves' approval for the way I went about my training.

"If you continue to improve as you are doing each day, Madame Fletcher, you should do well in next year's St. Cécile Ladies Downhill race. It is unfortunate that this year it is too late to enter you for the event, for the competition would be good for you."

His words encouraged me, and that night, for the third night in a row, I went to bed physically exhausted and blissfully sleepy.

Marguerite looked glum when she joined me for breakfast.

"I'm afraid we are going to be snowbound here for the next few hours," she grimaced. "Maurice won't be able to clear the drive until the snow stops, and in any case, there has been a warning on the local radio that some minor roads are blocked, the snow ploughs are out trying to keep the major roads clear, and people are advised not to travel unless it is really necessary." She sighed. "It's just my luck, isn't it? I had arranged to meet Edouard in Geneva to-day as we both have business meetings there, but it would be asking for trouble to make the trip. If this weather continues, Luke is not going to get any ski-ing practice this week-end, and that won't please him," she grimaced. "The weather is one of the few things he can't manipulate to suit his purpose.

There was no way Jamie could have got to school, but he didn't mind the unexpected holiday. I was disappointed when Yves 'phoned to confirm there would be no ski session that afternoon although I had guessed this might happen. As the snow flakes piled higher and higher on the window ledges I became more and more restless, experiencing again the frightening sensation of claustrophobia, or had it been the premonition of something direful about to happen, which had overwhelmed me in the Paris Métro that October day when a man had stepped to his death from the very spot where Jamie and I had been standing moments earlier.

I shivered at the memory and wished that Luke was here with me to assure me that it was my vivid imagination and nothing else which made me certain that something ominous was brewing, yet Luke's arrival, later that afternoon, gave me no such reassurance.

The snow had stopped at mid-day, we learned that the road to St. Cécile had been cleared, but it was still impossible to get the cars from the Château garages because the snow had drifted half way up against the doors and almost to roof level in places, and lay a foot deep in the yard and down the driveway, where there were also lesser drifting near the gateway.

In spite of this, Giselle was determined to get to Grenoble to bring Jean-Claude home for the week-end — and kept hounding poor old Maurice to hurry and clear the snow away, a job which would have taken a couple of younger and stronger men at least two hours to do, but Jamie willingly offered to help and with nothing more urgent to occupy ourselves with, Marguerite and I joined in.

It was almost four o'clock when we eventually succeeded in making it possible to get the cars out and the driveway cleared as far as the main road. Jamie, Marguerite and I were on our way back from the gateway, indulging in a good humoured snowball fight before returning to the house, when Giselle, who had been watching our endeavours from her window, came down the driveway in her car, giving us her 'great lady' smile and an almost condescending wave of thanks for our efforts.

Marguerite who, like me, was sticky and hot and flushed from what had been hard work, remarked angrily.

"You would think she was a real de la Haie and we, the family serfs, when she is nothing but a trumped up, third rate actress who married to get a title."

"I wouldn't say third rate," I grinned. "You must admit she plays the role she has chosen to perfection."

Marguerite sniffed and lobbed a snowball at me. I stepped out of the way and fell back into a heap of snow. Jamie tried to pull me to my feet, but slipped on top of me, and we were lying giggling when Marguerite exclaimed in surprise.

"Lisa, Luke's car is turning in at the gateway. I didn't know he was coming home this afternoon?"

"Nor did I!" I gasped, scrambling awkwardly to my feet as Luke, a broad grin on his face, brought the car to a halt alongside me. My eyes sparkled with delight till I saw Frédérique was beside him wearing the smile of a cat who has stolen the cream.

Jamie rushed to welcome his uncle, then pouted crossly, "What's she doing here? Did her car break down again so that you could drive her?"

Behind me Marguerite stifled a snort of laughter, but Frédérique was not amused and gasped angrily, "What impertinence!"

"Jamie," Luke spoke sternly. "That was most impolite. Apologise to Frédérique at once."

Jamie flushed but refused to speak.

"Jamie, you heard me. Say you are sorry."

For a second he hesitated, but Luke's angry expression made him mutter a quick 'Sorry' before, scowling, he turned and limped away.

"You must be more strict with him, Lisa," snapped Frédérique. "He has been getting out of hand recently."

"Nonsense." Marguerite still not on the best of terms with the partner who had let her down with her most important clients, looked coldly at the other woman. "There is nothing wrong with Jamie. He is a natural small boy who behaves like all small boys. Luke was the same at his age, and you seem to approve of the way he has turned out."

With that, she opened the back door of Luke's car and urged me in ahead of her, saying as she did so, in none too welcoming a tone, "What are you doing here, by the way?"

"There was something wrong with the clutch of Frédérique's car," Luke explained, his expression still annoyed. "Naturally when she asked me to, I offered to drive her home from Cannes. I had meant to take her to her own house before coming here, but we were told the road to her village on the other side of the pass is still blocked, which means she will have to spend the night at Les Neiges."

"It will be just like old times, won't it?" Frédérique gave me a sly look.

"Hardly," retorted Marguerite drily.

"Luke is married now and Lisa has converted the former guest room into a study, so I'm afraid you will have to sleep elsewhere. Giselle hasn't a guest room in her wing, but I am sure, if you ask Jamie nicely, he will allow you to occupy the blue room in the main building."

"Ask Jamie?" she gaped at Marguerite. "What do you mean?"

"Until the plans for the hotel are finalised, he owns the Château. We lease our wing from him, as does Giselle. There he is," she wound down the window as she caught sight of the boy mounting the steps to the massive front door, "We can ask him now."

Jamie, however, pretended not to hear, and disappeared into the building.

Marguerite shrugged. "Perhaps it is just as well we didn't ask at the moment. He is obviously not in the best of moods with us." She turned to me. "Lisa, later on, would you have a word with him? He likes obliging you."

I could sense a tension in the air.

Frédérique was furious at the way things were working out, and for some reason, Luke, too, was not in the best of humours. This atmosphere ruined Luke's homecoming for me, or perhaps it was Frédérique's unwanted presence which did this. She hovered beside Luke, even knocking on the bedroom door where I had gone to help him unpack, to call out that perhaps it might be more suitable if she spent the night in the village inn, since she seemed to be such a nuisance.

Luke glanced at me and sighed. "Frédérique seems to think you don't like her and object to having her come here. Perhaps you ought to go along to Jamie now, and tell him that Frédérique will be spending the night in the guest room at the end of the corridor where his room is, and will be sharing his bathroom."

I found Jamie lying on the window seat in the playroom, his head pillowed on his pet cat's warm, soft, purring body. I knew that when he was upset it was often to Snoopy he turned for consolation, and to-day, Luke's annoyance, and the fact he had had to apologise to someone he disliked, had upset him deeply.

He wasn't at all pleased when I told him about Frédérique.

"I don't like her and she doesn't like me. I don't see why she has to spend the night here."

"It is just one night," I replied, stroking Snoopy, "and there will be no need for you to take your bath toys from the bathroom. After all, it is your bathroom and you are doing her a favour letting her use it."

"I can leave all my toys there?" he grinned suddenly, and the malicious look on his face made me remember about the plastic snake which had given me the fright of my life when it had come slithering down the cold tap the first night I had supervised his bath. I found myself grinning too, and hoping that it would give Frédérique an even bigger fright.

I was in no hurry to return to Frédérique's company, so I helped Nana prepare the blue room, chatted to her for a time while she prepared a light supper for Jamie, and went back to the playroom to say goodnight to Jamie, but he wasn't there. Nor was there anyone in our living room when I returned to our wing, which made me frown and wonder what was going on. Then the sound of the dinner gong made me realise it was much later than I had thought. The others had gone ahead of me for the usual pre-dinner drinks. I felt peeved because Luke hadn't waited as I quickly changed into a pretty wool frock which Luke liked, and went hurrying to the dining room. No doubt he had been so engrossed with Frédérique's flirtative company he had forgotten about me.

Giselle frowned as I entered the candle-lit dining room.

"Where is Luke?" she demanded. "Is he still chasing that wild cat?"

"What wild cat?"

"Jamie's, of course. I am sure he

chased it down the main stairway on purpose as I was crossing the hall, and I nearly fell over it. I screamed at it and it disappeared towards the kitchen. Then Jamie came running down afraid it might get outside and Luke went to help him find it. I told him he shouldn't. It would be the best thing if the animal escaped. Cats should be kept in stables, not houses, and that's where this one would be if I had my way."

"Which unfortunately you can't have," put in Frédérique who had been none too pleased that I was the one who had had to intercede with Jamie to allow her to stay overnight at Les Neiges. "It's Jamie's cat and it's Jamie's Castle and he can do what he pleases here."

Luke came into the room, an amused smile on his face.

"Snoopy caught a mouse in the cellar and is now in cook's good books. Jamie is delighted because Snoopy was so clever, and Snoopy is happy because she has been given a piece of chicken as a reward, so all's well that ends well."

Luke had told me that ski-ing was his first love, and the fortnight that followed, I learned it was still a love of his life, for when he wasn't at work in his office he was on the mountains, practising for the championship.

There was much excitement when the great day arrived. Marguerite, Luke and Jean Claude left together, all three determined to win the events for which they had entered. Nana, Jamie and I left later, to go to the course and take up our position on the high bank near the foot of the run, which Jean Claude had told us was the best vantage point for spectators. I glimpsed Frédérique close by, but she pretended not to see us, which pleased us all.

It was a superb day, and the ski-ing was equally superb. Jamie and I shouted and cheered as the competitors hurtled down the course at incredible speeds, taking difficult corners and humps with incredible competence. There were several falls to add to the excitement, but no one was badly hurt. Marguerite came second in her event, ceding first place to the European Women's Champion, but the main event was the men's race. Jean Claude broke his own record time, but it was Luke who beat him with the last run, by the fraction of a second.

We were hurrying to congratulate him when someone tripped me up. By the time I got to my feet, Frédérique was standing beside Luke, giving him a congratulatory hug and kiss, turning with him to face the photographers, her arm round his waist.

I stood still with indignation. How dare she. Then Jamie and Nana were urging me forward, and seeing me, Luke released himself from Frédérique's possessive hold and came to me, smiling, saying, "Aren't you proud of me, darling?"

"Of course," I kissed his glowing cheek, "but I knew you would win.

I'm told the de la Haies always get what they want."

"We do, don't we?" he grinned, giving Jamie a friendly punch on the shoulder. "To celebrate, I've arranged something special, but just for Lisa and me," he smiled at the boy. "You have to stay at home and keep an eye on Marguerite and Nana for me, while Lisa and I spend a few days in Nice for the Carnival. I promised you that holiday, Lisa, and I keep my promises."

Frédérique darted me a malevolent glance, but I could afford to ignore her actions. She had been trying to stir up trouble and failing. She hadn't managed to undermine my faith in Luke and she never would.

Everything seemed to be going my way for the moment. I was going with Luke to Nice. The tenants of Les Narcisses were moving out a week earlier than expected, which meant I could get work started on my future home on my return from my short holiday, and hopefully we would be able to move in by mid May. My agent had written to say he was certain he would be able to place my travel book. I was on top of the world and fortunately couldn't guess how soon I was to be toppled down.

I was thrilled with the drive down the Route Napoleon through Gap and Sisteron, with magnificent snowy mountain scenery all around. The snow gradually disappeared the nearer we drew to the coast, then I caught sight of my first red-roofed Provençal houses, my first olive tree, smelt the perfume of the golden mimosas which grew in abundance along the last miles of the journey, and then we were in Nice, where even the colourful flower beds and the palm trees were lit up for the Carnival, which would reach its culmination in three days.

Our hotel, the Negresco, overlooked the Promenade des Anglais and the Baie des Anges, and from our bedroom window I took more photographs, of the view, of the crowds, of the palm trees so different from the pines surrounding St. Cécile. That night and next day we joined with the revellers in the streets, throwing confetti and flowers and wandering arm in arm, sometimes humming the catchy carnival songs, sometimes joining in the impromptu dancing. I floated in a bubble of happiness, a bubble which was pricked the next morning.

Luke was having a shower when the 'phone rang. It was Marguerite.

"Lisa, I hate to bother you, but we are having problems with Jamie. He won't go to school, he won't go into the village, he won't even leave the Château. He's having his dreadful nightmares again and in his sleep he cries for his mother."

"What started all this? There must be something."

"He says he saw that man who broke into his bedroom in the village. He insists he was driving the same car that ran over his sledge at the leisure centre. He thinks the man wants to hurt him, and he is scared. He may be imagining things, Lisa, but it all seems very real to him and Nana and I are at our wits' end."

My blood ran cold as she was speaking. I remembered all too vividly the day the sledge had been broken, aware still that if it hadn't been for Yves, we might have been killed. I had thought Jamie unaffected by the incident, too excited over his new sledge to think of it, but fear had been there, lurking at the back of his mind, brought to the surface when he saw and recognised that car again. I had no doubt he was right about the car, but as to his recognition of the man, that was unlikely, though I could understand his mistake. Two frightening incidents had fused in his mind. Small wonder his nightmares had started again. Small wonder he started at shadows.

There was only one thing to do. He needed Luke. He even needed me for reassurance. We would have to return to St. Cécile, and Luke agreed.

Marguerite and Nana were thankful to see us, and for days Jamie was fearful of letting us out of his sight. Eventually we got him to return to school, but someone had to accompany him and bring him home, and I was the one he wanted to be with him. His anxiety when he was in the village was contagious and I too found myself glancing over my shoulder at times, certain someone was spying on us.

This unusual nervousness, the excitement of working and planning in my new home, keeping an eye on Jamie, and the unbelievable thrill of having my book accepted conspired to make me feel as I used to feel before examinations or important interviews, queasy and a bit below par. I was almost relieved when Luke said he had to go to Paris for a week to deal with some further problems to do with the change over of the château from private residence to hotel, hoping I would feel myself again before he returned home, but the knowledge that Frédérique was going to Paris that same week and had arranged, as she had arranged at Cannes, to reserve a room in the hotel where he would be staying, set my nerves on edge anew.

Luke's trip to Paris had been successful and again all seemed to be going well for us. The decorators finished on time and we were able to move in to Les Narcisses on the fifteenth of May as planned. I arranged a house-warming party, but even with Marguerite's help, I was tired and nervous when the time came to welcome our first guests. Jamie, naturally was at the party and he kept the guests entertained, telling them how he had chosen the decorations for his own room and how he had frightened the decorators with his plastic snake. He then said that his present to me for the house-warming was that he was going to take me to a very special place next day, a place his mother had loved, and which they had called gentian valley.

"Wait until the week-end, Jamie," said Luke. "I can go with you then. The road to the valley is dangerous at the moment, especially where the snow hasn't yet melted. It is very steep and twisty and Lisa might not enjoy driving on it."

"I want to show her it tomorrow," said Jamie mutinously. "She's a good driver."

I wanted no arguments. I decided it was time Jamie went to bed, and I went with him to his room, waited to tuck him in, with Snoopy by his side, then assured him that if the weather was fine, we would go together to his special valley in the morning. I saw no reason why I shouldn't. I had made my own decisions before I was married and I was still capable of doing so.

In no hurry to rejoin my guests or watch Frédérique follow Luke around like a shadow, I slipped into the library for a few moments on my own. I went to the window, sat down on the high backed chair I had strategically placed to command a view of the valley, and gazed out at the distant mountains.

The door opened. I heard Frédérique's voice, saw her, in the pale reflection of the window, put her arms round Luke and embrace him passionately. Too taken aback to be able to move, I sat immobile, and heard them talk together, heard words which told me my dream was over; heard Luke tell Frédérique, as, with his arm round her waist he urged her out of the room, that there was only one woman for him; only one woman he had ever truly loved, and then the door closed behind them.

I sat for a long time. I felt sick. I felt desolate. I wondered what I should do, then decided there was only one thing I could do. I must leave Les Narcisses; leave Luke to the love of his life. I would go tomorrow. No, not tomorrow. I had promised Jamie I would go to his valley with him tomorrow, and I wouldn't break that promise, but once we returned to the villa, I would pack and go.

How I behaved naturally for the remainder of the evening I don't know, but when the guests had left and only the family, only Marguerite and Giselle, Jean Claude and the omnipresent Frédérique remained, still sipping champagne and talking animatedly, I pleaded a migraine and went up to bed.

I pretended to be asleep, and when Luke bent over me, and shook me, mumbled grumpily I felt awful and would he sleep in the dressing room?

I pretended to be still suffering from migraine when he left for work in the morning. I did feel physically nauseated for a time, so I wasn't actually telling a lie. He looked at me oddly, almost as if he suspected I was up to something, then kissed my forehead lightly and left.

I waited until he drove away before dressing and joining Nana and Jamie for breakfast. After we had eaten, I told Nana that Jamie and I were going to see his gentian valley. "It's a special treat he is giving me."

"It is that. It's a beautiful place, but have a care, Mrs. Fletcher. It's a very tricky road."

"I'll take my time. There won't be much traffic so early."

Luke and Nana were right about the road. It was gravel surfaced, steep, narrow and very tortuous, conditions varying from dry to slippery and snowy as we twisted round shadowy overhangs. I had to concentrate on the road ahead and didn't become aware that there was a car behind me until it nudged my bumpers, jolting us.

I glanced in my mirror to glare at the careless driver. Jamie looked round too and exclaimed shrilly, "Lisa. That's the car that ran over my sledge. It's the same man driving it and," his voice rose in surprise, "Grand'mère is with him!"

"Oh!" I breathed with relief. "Then it's all right. He will be a friend of

229

Giselle. That's why you recognised his face."

"But why are they here?"

"Last night, after you left, Giselle said she would like to see your valley. Gentians are her favourite flowers."

"I don't want her to see my valley," Jamie pouted. "It spoils things, her being here."

Giselle's driver was certainly spoiling things the way he kept trying to overtake, an insane maneouvre on such a road. The first time he tried he bumped against our rear wheels, making me skid towards the edge and a horrifying drop to the river bed far, far below. A misjudgement, I thought, as I accelerated out of trouble, but his second attempt was too deliberate to be accidental, for he came alongside and forcefully bumped his car against ours, although there was plenty of room on his side.

I turned to glare at him, caught sight of Giselle's face staring at me, contorted with hatred and knew for certain, then, that they were intending to send us crashing to our deaths. I didn't take time to wonder why. Although fear made my hands clammy on the steering wheel, it made my brain work fast. I accelerated again out of harm's way, going much too fast for the road conditions, but keeping ahead was our only way of escape. I am no Rally driver, but somehow I kept on going, keeping to the centre and as often as not half over on the wrong side of the road, to prevent our pursuers from overtaking.

Jamie, fortunately didn't realise what was happening. "We'll get there first," he crowed. "It's just round the next bend. You will see a lay-by just before the hairpin after this one. It's at the top of the goat track which leads to the valley. The track isn't wide enough for a car," he added.

A lay-by. A goat track. I doubted if my pursuers knew about them. I rounded the first corner, coming to a straight stretch, spotted the lay-by which my car concealed from the car behind. I moved to the left. The car behind was quick to try to overtake. I accelerated. The other driver did too, and prepared to ram me, but he wasn't prepared for my next move. I stood on the brakes and skidded into the layby, while he went flying past, seeing his danger too late. He struggled to steer back on course, but it was too late. The corner was too close. It was Giselle's car, not mine, that went over the side.

Jamie screamed. I moved to put my arm round him. It was a disastrous move. Our car, itself dangerously close to the drop, slipped sideways. The lip of the lay-by, soft and crumbly after the weight of winter snow, gave way under the side wheels. In horrifying slow motion the Fiat fell over on its side and went rolling over and over down the steep track, scraping and bumping on outcrops until with a final somersault it came to rest wedged between the two precipitous cliffs, which formed the narrow passage into gentian valley.

Our seat belts had saved us from being flung around, but now I felt shaky inside. My door wouldn't open, but Jamie's did, and we both managed to drop from it some ten feet onto the springy softness of clumps of alpenroses. We were hugging ourselves in our relief when I heard someone screaming.

"It's grandmother," exclaimed Jamie. "She is over there somewhere."

I put my hand firmly on his shoulder. "You stay here, Jamie. Here is my scarf. It is red and will show up well if you wave it. From this spot you can be seen from the road, and we shall need help, the sooner the better."

He hesitated, then decided to obey and stood, slowly waving the scarf while I gingerly made my way over the rough, steep terrain in the direction of the screaming. I sidled round a great boulder and along a cliff face, then stopped to stare up at a pine tree which grew horizontally from a widish ledge on the face of the cliff. Giselle had been flung from the car and by a fluke had been caught and held by the branches. She was now awkwardly inching her way along the trunk to the ledge, screaming all the time.

I couldn't reach her. She would have to be rescued from the road by someone with a rope. She reached the ledge and looked down as I called to her.

"Are you hurt?"

"Philippe is dead," she screamed at me. "He went down with the car. I heard it crash. He couldn't have survived and it's your fault."

"My-my fault?" I was startled by her words.

"If it hadn't been for you he would be alive, but somehow you were always there to thwart us and save Jamie."

"Save Jamie?" I repeated her words parrot fashion.

"Yes, Jamie, the little cripple who stood between Jean Claude and everything I wanted for him. Don't you understand, if Jamie had only died in the crash with his parents, Jean Claude would have become the Count de la Haie. He would have inherited the Château and we would have kept it as a private home, a home fit for the brilliant politician he will be."

"You are mad!" I stared at her in horror.

"Ambitious for my son, not mad," she denied the charge. "The idea came when I was standing at Alain's graveside, thinking how his father had cheated me by not telling me he already had a son when I married him. Then I realised that only a little boy stood between me and what I had expected to get from that marriage, a little boy I hated. Hated," she repeated. "Over the years I'd paid my brother, with his criminal background, to stay out of my life. Now I would pay him to do a job for me. I — " she stopped and looked, as I was now looking, at the mountain which overhung gentian valley. The cliff face above the road was disintegrating. Snow, ice, scree and rubble began to move downwards, gathering speed as terrified, I scrambled round the boulder and back the way I had come to see Jamie, right in the path of the avalanche, stare up at it petrified.

I got to him, grabbed him, hauled him to the hopeful safety of a fissure under the cliff beside which our car was wedged. As I pushed him in under a hail of small stones, my shoulder was struck with a force which sent me staggering in after him.

We sat there for almost an hour listening to the avalanche pass, afraid to move in case we started another one. Finally my claustrophobia drove me into the open. All that now could be seen of Jamie's lovely gentian valley was a wedge of blue amid a mass of rubble and boulders. I shivered, no one would guess we had survived such a landfall, even if our car was seen from the road, but I couldn't just stand doing nothing.

Painfully I hauled myself over the debris to a pile of rock and pulled myself half up it. Stopping for breath I looked up. A car, no doubt stopped by the landfall, was parked near the top of the goat track. I shouted and waved. A man's voice called back.

"Lisa! Mon Dieu! Are you all right?"

"Luke!" I couldn't believe my eyes. "We're safe. We are both safe, but Giselle — "

"We found her. She said you had been killed."

She had hoped we would be killed. Then she would have won for there was no one, not even her brother, who would have been alive to betray what she had been up to.

Luke made his way cautiously down what remained of the track. I tried to pull myself higher up over the pile of rocks. I heard Jamie come behind me. In my effort to pull myself as near to Luke as I could, my fingers dislodged a small rock. It fell away, striking the side of my head before I had time to dodge it, and next thing I was aware of was lying on the roadside with Luke bending over me.

"I still can't believe you are real," I said stupidly. "How did you get here?"

"I'm real enough," he put his arm round me, "and I got here because when I left you this morning there was an evasive look in your eyes which made me think you were up to something you didn't think I would approve of. It wasn't until someone in the office mentioned last night's party I realised what it might be. I drop home to have Nana confirm that you and Jamie had gone off to gentian valley. You little idiot," he spoke angrily. "I warned you the road was dangerous."

"We weren't in any danger from my driving. We are here because Giselle forced us off the road. She was the danger."

"What the devil do you mean?"

Jamie wasn't to be seen, so I told him what had happened, heard him gasp angrily as, at the end of the recital, pain and weakness made me close my eyes and moan. I could have sworn his lips kissed my eyelids, but what did it matter? Nothing mattered now, knowing I had lost him.

The scream of a siren half roused me, its blue light hurt my lids. I was picked up, tried to open my eyes, but blessed oblivion took over.

9

THE nightmare kept recurring. I was in a car, falling, falling, and Jamie was by my side. Then we were on a rocky hillside running desperately for the safety of a fissure in the cliff as snow and rocks came thundering towards us. I was frightened, so frightened that I forced myself to wake up and found my pillow and the clothes I was wearing soaked with sweat.

I became conscious of voices murmuring nearby. Unaccustomed smells assailed my nostrils. The smell of ether, of antiseptics, of hospitals. I opened my eyes and stared up at a white ceiling. I felt the hardness of a strange bed beneath me. I had a growing awareness of an aching shoulder and a throbbing pain behind my ear, which increased when I moved my head.

Dr. de Vigny's tall figure came into view, then his face, looking anxiously down at me.

"Where am I?What happened?" I tried to sit up but he put a hand on my uninjured shoulder and held me down.

"Take it easy, Madame Fletcher. There was an accident. You are in hospital."

I shuddered. My mind was clearing. Now I knew my nightmare had been a reality, but Dr. de Vigny was wrong. What had happened hadn't been an accident, but attempted murder, yet I mustn't say that. I had come to for a few minutes in the ambulance, to find Luke beside me. He had whispered urgently that for everyone's sake what happened must be accepted as an accident.

"It's a lot to ask of you chérie, but we want nothing to come out that would give the yellow press a headline, for Jamie's sake. He didn't realise exactly what was going on. We don't want him ever to find out that that woman tried to have him killed. He has had enough traumas in his young life. The story, as far as the world is concerned, is that both cars skidded on frozen snow and went over the edge. It is the truth. Only you and I, Giselle and Marguerite know that it is not the whole truth."

The whole truth. He was right. That was too awful for Jamie ever to know about. I shuddered again and Dr. de Vigny took hold of my hand and held it gently.

"You must forget what might have happened, my dear. You are alive. Now you must look to the future. I can assure you that everything is going to be all right," he looked pleased with himself. "You have been given a thorough check over. There are no broken bones, no internal injuries. You have a lot of bruising. Your shoulder will ache for some time as will the bump on your head, but yes," again he gave me that pleased smile, "everything else is all right. You didn't lose the baby."

"The baby?" Again I tried to sit up.

He looked at me, surprised. "Didn't you know you were pregnant?"

The surge of delight his words had given me gave way to despair.

"I — I wasn't sure. I had been feeling off colour and sickish, but I get that way when I'm nervous or have too much on my mind. I had hoped — " my voice trailed off.

He took me up wrongly. "You were afraid your hopes might be dashed? You wanted to be sure before you came to me?"

I closed my eyes. I couldn't look at him. How could I tell this kindly man that I had hoped my suspicions were wrong? How could I tell him that much as I wanted Luke's child, it would not be right to have it, for a child would keep him from marrying the woman he loved and should have married in the first place.

243

He stood up. "I'm glad I gave you some good news. You will be eager to let Luke know, I daresay, so I shall give you the 'phone number where you can contact him in Geneva, once you get back to Les Narcisses. There is no need to keep you here in hospital, and your sister-in-law should be here at any moment to take you home."

"Have you told her about the baby?" I asked sharply.

"Of course not," he seemed taken aback. "I thought you would want your husband to be the first to have the news confirmed."

I twisted the sheet nervously with my fingers and looked up at him, puzzled, only now taking in what he had said about Geneva.

"What's Luke doing in Geneva?" I stared at him. "Why — "

"Why did he go, when you were here?" he finished the question for me, and shook his head. "Poor man, he had to make up his mind. Who needed him most? You or Jamie. The doctor who came with you in the ambulance had assured him he was certain you had no serious injuries, whereas Jamie — "

"Jamie?" I interrupted. "What happened to Jamie? I thought I'd got him out of the way in time."

"He was scrambling up to the road after the men who were carrying you, when he fell and tumbled back down, breaking his leg again. He was beside himself at the thought of having to go to hospital here, where he had been before, with rather unhappy results, so Luke chartered a helicopter and had him taken to the best clinic in Switzerland, where this time a leading surgeon, not a student, will set his leg for him. Your husband went with him. He was sure you would understand."

"Yes," I tried not to sound sorry for myself. "Of course he couldn't have let Jamie go on his own."

There was a tap on the door. Marguerite came into the room.

"I'm not too early, am I?"

"No, no. The nurse will help

Madame Fletcher dress, then you may take her home, but remember," he turned to me, "you must rest in bed for a few days. It's important. Nana and your sister-in-law will look after you, so you will be in good hands. I myself will call to see you at the end of the week."

Marguerite put her arm round me when she helped me out to her car, and there was affection in her voice as she said.

"I know I'm no substitute for Luke, but I'll do my best to keep an eye on you until he returns."

I sat back exhaustedly in the seat. My body ached, I was painfully conscious of every bump along the way and had to concentrate on keeping myself from crying out, but when we reached Les Narcisses, where the lights from the downstairs room shone out into the darkness, I touched Marguerite's hand.

"Now, when we are alone, tell me. What happened to Giselle?"

"She has gone. Luke told her, for

the sake of the family, there would be no charges laid against her, but he isn't a fool, Lisa. He made her sign a confession about her attempts to murder Jamie, in Paris, in the Château, and of course, to-day. If Jamie has any more 'accidents' he will hand the confession to the police."

"Lisa, he frightened me, the way he looked at her as she was writing. He frightened her, too, which is why she packed and went so quickly."

"She deserves to be more than frightened," I said angrily. "She deserves to be punished."

"She has been punished," Marguerite spoke slowly. "She has to live with the knowledge that she was responsible for the deaths of two men. Her cousin was the man who tried to push Jamie under the train in Paris and fell to his own death instead. Her brother was the man Jamie surprised in his bedroom the first night you were in the Château, and who tried on at least two other occasions, apart from to-day, to kill him. He was the chauffeur.

"She has also lost her son," she went on with satisfaction.

"Jean Claude? Did he know what his mother was up to?"

"No. He would have put a stop to it. He is very fond of Jamie, as you know. In any case, he has no great ambitions. He doesn't give a damn about having a title or a rambling castle to call home. All he wants to do is to ski and swim and climb and play tennis, and that's what he is going to do.

"Last night after you went to bed with your migraine, Luke offered him a job as a member of the Château Hotel team. He is to be assistant to Luke on the sport and leisure side, ski instructing, tennis coaching, arranging walks and climbs, that sort of thing. He is also to take a course in hotel management. It's a job tailored for him. He accepted without even looking towards his mother for her approval, and she was furious. He thinks she

248

took off to-day to show her displeasure with him, and he isn't at all upset. I believe he is delighted that she won't be around to interfere in his life.

"But I've spoken enough. Into the house and up to bed with you, Lisa. I'll come with you and make sure you take the pills de Vigny gave me to give to you to ensure a good night's sleep."

For the next few days I slept and rested and ate the meals Nana prepared specially for me. I followed de Vigny's advice in all but one thing. I didn't tell Luke about the baby. I wanted time to think, though thinking made my head ache. My body ached less, I felt stronger each day, yet I was reluctant to leave the safe cocoon of my bed and face the outside world.

As he had promised, Dr. de Vigny came to visit me at the end of the week. "It's time you were on your feet again," he told me. "Get up for a little this afternoon, then a little longer each day, but no climbing or ski-ing for the time being."

249

"How about flower arranging?" I tried to joke.

He smiled. "I might even allow you to pull a flower or two. Fresh air will be good for you. It will put some colour back in your cheeks before your husband comes home, which should be soon, for I am told Jamie's leg is mending well and he is being spoilt in the clinic."

He said goodbye and left me. I listened to his footsteps grow fainter as he went down the wooden staircase. If only there was a doctor who could mend broken hearts as well as broken legs, I sighed drearily as I cautiously swung my legs over the side of the bed and walked slowly across to the window.

In the few days I had been in bed, the long sweep of meadow from the house to the road had changed from a swathe of dark green to a white carpet of the sweetly scented flowers from which the villa derived its name.

A week ago the sight would have

entranced me. To-day I could only feel sad. I would have to put all this loveliness, the home I had hoped to make for Luke and our children and Jamie, behind me. I would not cling to a husband who did not want me. I crept back to bed overcome with a tiredness which was emotional rather than physical.

I was pulling the duvet over me when the door opened. I expected to see Marguerite. It was Luke who strode into the room, on his face an expression of such delight that I was taken aback.

He came to the bed, caught hold of my hands and held them firmly.

"Lisa, Dr. de Vigny has been telling me about the baby. He was as surprised as I was when he learned you hadn't told me the news."

I took a deep breath.

"It was something I didn't want to have to tell you, Luke. It shouldn't have happened. It will make things difficult."

He stared at me in disbelief. "Lisa, you can't mean that you don't want our child," his grasp was now so tight I winced. "You love children. You told me Les Narcisses would be a wonderful home for a family. You even planned a nursery — oh yes," he went on, seeing the startled look in my eyes, "I saw the papers and curtains you had marked off in Marguerite's book of patterns. And you're so good with Jamie, too," he frowned. "What has made you change your mind? Are you afraid?"

"No," I sighed, "I'm not afraid. But surely you must understand that I don't want a child to bind you to a marriage that should not have taken place."

"What the devil do you mean?" he gaped in surprise.

"Don't pretend. I know about you and Frédérique. I know you would have married her if she had been willing to accept Jamie, which she didn't want to do. I know you still love her and that now she wants you enough to marry you, Jamie or no Jamie. No,"

252

I pulled a hand free and covered his mouth to stop him interrupting, "don't deny it. Don't lie for the sake of the baby. I was there in the study the night before the accident. I was in the high backed chair at the window and neither of you saw me, but I saw the way she kissed you, the way she clung to you, and I didn't want to be humiliated by letting her know of my presence, so I sat still, and then I heard her say she still loved you and would marry you on any terms. That she had been foolish to walk out on you because of Jamie and it wasn't fair you should both pay for a mistake which could be remedied. A marriage of convenience such as yours was no marriage."

I paused for breath and felt tears trickle down my cheeks, saw them fall on his hands, wanted this moment to be over quickly.

"Lisa, you've got it wrong," Luke shook his head.

"Have I?" I half sobbed. "No, no. I saw you put your arm round her waist and say to her as you led her from the room, 'There has only been one woman I have ever wanted to marry, Frédérique. Only one woman I love.' Then you closed the door, and I was left, so alone, so sad, knowing our marriage was just a convenience; knowing you still loved her and wanted her."

Luke drew a long breath.

"Mon Dieu!" he reverted to French in his exasperation. "So that's why you behaved so oddly that night; why you went up to bed early, pleading a migraine, and packed me off to the dressing room for the night. You little idiot," he put his hand on my shoulder caressingly, "if only you had heard the rest of the conversation you would have been spared days of misery," he studied my woebegone face, "And I would have been spared the shock of being told that you didn't want my child.

"Lisa, Lisa," he was looking at me with such tenderness that the coldness which had been round my heart melted and the warmth of relief and sheer happiness flooded through my veins, "if only you had heard me tell Frédérique I was tired of the way she kept hanging around me, even pushing you aside from me, usurping your place, as she did at the Championship. If only you had heard me tell her the only woman in my life is you and that the only woman I have ever truly loved is you," he shook his head, "but surely you knew that? How could we have been what we were to each other, friends, lovers, so contented when we were together, if I hadn't loved you.

"Darling," his hand touched my cheek, thrilling me with renewed emotion, "I love you for your smile and your enthusiasm about the things you do. I love you because you are what you are, a romantic and an idealist. I have loved you from the moment I saw you so eager to catch a golden autumn leaf, to bring you luck."

He sat on the bed and took me in his arms, to hold me close, kissing my face, my neck, my bruised shoulder with a tenderness which was more loving than any passionate embrace, pausing only once between the kisses to say the words I had so wanted to hear.

"I love you, Lisa. Now and for always, so never, never, my darling, doubt that love again."

THE END

WITH SOMEBODY ELSE
Theresa Charles

Rosamond sets off for Cornwall with Hugo to meet his family, blissfully unaware of the shocks in store for her.

A SUMMER FOR STRANGERS
Claire Hamilton

Because she had lost her job, her flat and she had no money, Tabitha agreed to pose as Adam's future wife although she believed the scheme to be deceitful and cruel.

VILLA OF SINGING WATER
Angela Petron

The disquieting incidents that occurred at the Vatican and the Colosseum did not trouble Jan at first, but then they became increasingly unpleasant and alarming.

DOCTOR NAPIER'S NURSE
Pauline Ash

When cousins Midge and Derry are entered as probationer nurses on the same day but at different hospitals they agree to exchange identities.

A GIRL LIKE JULIE
Louise Ellis

Caroline absolutely adored Hugh Barrington, but then Julie Crane came into their lives. Julie was the kind of girl who attracts men without even trying.

COUNTRY DOCTOR
Paula Lindsay

When Evan Richmond bought a practice in a remote country village he did not realise that a casual encounter would lead to the loss of his heart.

ENCORE
Helga Moray

Craig and Janet realise that their true happiness lies with each other, but it is only under traumatic circumstances that they can be reunited.

NICOLETTE
Ivy Preston

When Grant Alston came back into her life, Nicolette was faced with a dilemma. Should she follow the path of duty or the path of love?

THE GOLDEN PUMA
Margaret Way

Catherine's time was spent looking after her father's Queensland farm. But what life was there without David, who wasn't interested in her?

HOSPITAL BY THE LAKE
Anne Durham

Nurse Marguerite Ingleby was always ready to become personally involved with her patients, to the despair of Brian Field, the Senior Surgical Registrar, who loved her.

VALLEY OF CONFLICT
David Farrell

Isolated in a hostel in the French Alps, Ann Russell sees her fiancé being seduced by a young girl. Then comes the avalanche that imperils their lives.

NURSE'S CHOICE
Peggy Gaddis

A proposal of marriage from the incredibly handsome and wealthy Reagan was enough to upset any girl — and Brooke Martin was no exception.

A DANGEROUS MAN
Anne Goring

Photographer Polly Burton was on safari in Mombasa when she met enigmatic Leon Hammond. But unpredictability was the name of the game where Leon was concerned.

PRECIOUS INHERITANCE
Joan Moules

Karen's new life working for an authoress took her from Sussex to a foreign airstrip and a kidnapping; to a real life adventure as gripping as any in the books she typed.

VISION OF LOVE
Grace Richmond

When Kathy takes over the rundown country kennels she finds Alec Stinton, a local vet, very helpful. But their friendship arouses bitter jealousy and a tragedy seems inevitable.

CRUSADING NURSE
Jane Converse

It was handsome Dr. Corbett who opened Nurse Susan Leighton's eyes and who set her off on a lonely crusade against some powerful enemies and a shattering struggle against the man she loved.

WILD ENCHANTMENT
Christina Green

Rowan's agreeable new boss had a dream of creating a famous perfume using her precious Silverstar, but Rowan's plans were very different.

DESERT ROMANCE
Irene Ord

Sally agrees to take her sister Pam's place as La Chartreuse the dancer, but she finds out there is more to it than dyeing her hair red and looking like her sister.

HEART OF ICE
Marie Sidney

How was January to know that not only would the warmth of the Swiss people thaw out her frozen heart, but that she too would play her part in helping someone to live again?

LUCKY IN LOVE
Margaret Wood

Companion-secretary to wealthy gambler Laura Duxford, who lived in Monaco, seemed to Melanie a fabulous job. Especially as Melanie had already lost her heart to Laura's son, Julian.

NURSE TO PRINCESS JASMINE
Lilian Woodward

Nick's surgeon brother, Tom, performs an operation on an Arabian princess, and she invites Tom, Nick and his fiancé to Omander, where a web of deceit and intrigue closes about them.

THE WAYWARD HEART
Eileen Barry

Disaster-prone Katherine's nickname was "Kate Calamity", but her boss went too far with an outrageous proposal, which because of her latest disaster, she could not refuse.

FOUR WEEKS IN WINTER
Jane Donnelly

Tessa wasn't looking forward to meeting Paul Mellor again — she had made a fool of herself over him once before. But was Orme Jared's solution to her problem likely to be the right one?

SURGERY BY THE SEA
Sheila Douglas

Medical student Meg hadn't really wanted to go and work with a G.P. on the Welsh coast although the job had its compensations. But Owen Roberts was certainly not one of them!

HEAVEN

The new ... ... or of Marbeck ha ... een ... ... it was rather unfortun... ... when he arrived unexpectedly he found an uninvited guest, complete with stetson and high boots.

LOVE WILL COME
Sarah Devon

June Baker's boss was not really her idea of her ideal man, but when she went from third typist to boss's secretary overnight she began to change her mind.

ESCAPE TO ROMANCE
Kay Winchester

Oliver and Jean first met on Swale Island. They were both trying to begin their lives afresh, but neither had bargained for complications from the past.